#12

The Kapuskasing Kids

THE MITCHELL BROTHERS SERIES

#12

The Kapuskasing Kids

THE MITCHELL BROTHERS SERIES

Brian McFarlane

Fenn Publishing Company Ltd.
Bolton, Canada

THE KAPUSKASING KIDS
BOOK TWELVE IN THE MITCHELL BROTHERS SERIES
A Fenn Publishing Book / September 2006

Fenn Publishing Company Ltd.
Bolton, Ontario, Canada

Distributed in Canada by H.B. Fenn and Company Ltd.
Bolton, Ontario, Canada, L7E 1W2
www.hbfenn.com

We acknowledge the financial support of the Government of Canada through the Book
Publishing Industry Development Program (BPIDP) for our publishing activities.

Library and Archives Canada Cataloguing in Publication

McFarlane, Brian, 1931-
        Kapuskasing Kids / Brian McFarlane.

(The Mitchell Brothers series ; bk. 12)
ISBN-13: 978-1-55168-285-3
ISBN-10: 1-55168-285-0

        I. Title. II. Series: McFarlane, Brian, 1931- . Mitchell brothers series ;
bk. 12.

PS8575.F37K36 2006   jC813'.54   C2006-903767-1

THE KAPUSKASING KIDS

NOTE FROM THE AUTHOR

Can you imagine what it must be like to attend an NHL team's training camp? To be a rookie and make the team? To score a goal in your first NHL game?

In 1936, the Mitchell brothers, Max and Marty, were still too young to play in the NHL. But their cousins Bert and Barry weren't. They earned a chance to make their big-league dreams come true. The twin brothers from Kapuskasing in the North Country were discovered at a game that pitted one family against another—the Mitchells versus the McCoys. The Kapuskasing Kids played in an era when scouts moved from rink to rink seeking fresh talent for NHL teams. The two defencemen proved to be a perfect fit for the Toronto Maple Leafs.

But when one of the twins gives in to the temptations of the big city, gets into trouble and then mysteriously disappears, Max and Marty are called on to find him. At stake are the hockey careers of their NHL cousins—the Kapuskasing Kids.

Brian McFarlane

CHAPTER 1

THE MITCHELLS BATTLE
THE MC COYS

On a bitterly cold New Year's Day in 1936, there was plenty of hockey excitement at the Cobalt arena in northern Ontario. The featured game at the old barnboarded rink was a battle between two family teams—the Mitchells versus the McCoys. It was a unique annual event, one that attracted hundreds of fans to the frigid confines of the aging arena. The first game had been organized years earlier by Mighty Mike Mitchell, a former pro player in the National Hockey Association, a league that preceded the NHL. The 1936 edition of the famous rivalry would mark the 25th anniversary of the game.

"I thought it was a good way to raise money for the widows of miners who lost their lives digging for silver and cobalt," Mighty Mike explained to the dozen other Mitchells who were gathered around a pot-bellied stove, pulling on their hockey gear in a dressing room only slightly larger than a Siberian prison cell.

While Mighty Mike talked, he warmed his hands over the stove that stood in the centre of the room. "When I played pro for Cobalt back in 1910, I went down in the mines in the off-season," he continued, "and some good old boys got trapped in cave-ins and never came out. Two were Mitchells, and another was a McCoy. So we gather here every year, a few days after Christmas, to play this fundraising game. We raise some money for widows and orphans, and the event gives both families—the McCoys and the Mitchells—a chance to hold a family reunion."

"Because this is our 25th game," he went on, "and because the series is tied at 12 wins for each family, today's game is the most important one in the series. The town of Cobalt has promised to match the gate receipts today, and all the proceeds will go to the families of miners who perished below ground."

Mighty Mike's teenage nephews, Max and Marty Mitchell, had arrived in town the day before from their hometown of Indian River, 100 miles away. The brothers fidgeted on a bench in the dressing room. They were excited, thrilled to be invited to play for Team Mitchell for the first time. They had almost finished putting on their hockey uniforms, and listened attentively as Mighty Mike traced the history of the game.

"Some of the miners made huge fortunes here," he told his team. "And most of them have supported this game and been very generous when it comes to helping the families of those who died in the mines. Even those who got rich and moved away send me donations every year.

"This year the senior players on Team Mitchell decided to bring in some new blood for our game with the McCoys. I turned 50 the other day and my legs are shot. Some of the other Mitchells decided it was time to bow out. So I'll be coaching the team instead of playing. And I'm relying on some of you young pups in the Mitchell clan to help our creaking oldtimers. There'll be four new Mitchells in this year's lineup."

He turned to Max and Marty. "I want to thank you boys for giving up part of your Christmas vacation to be with us. Marty, you'll be our goalie in this year's game, and Max will be our starting centreman. I guess you've met all your relatives by now—they're all Mitchells."

"We sure have," Max said, looking around the room. "Some of you we've met before, but I've never played on a hockey team with no one but Mitchells on it."

"If they tried to broadcast the game on radio,

the announcer would have a breakdown," Marty quipped. He held up the blade of his hockey stick and talked into it. "'Mitchell—over to Mitchell—back to Mitchell. McCoy intercepts, over to McCoy—McCoy shoots! And Mitchell saves! I mean McCoy. No, it's Mitchell. And now McCoy...' See what I mean?"

The room erupted in laughter. "Good job, Marty," someone shouted.

"It's a great idea, Uncle Mike," said Max. "Holding a benefit game every year. And we're proud to be here. I thought you'd never get around to inviting us."

"Well, there's a reason for that," Mighty Mike explained. "We're playing the McCoys, you know. And over the years the rivalry has become bitter. Sometimes things threaten to get out of hand. I didn't want you getting hurt. But now you're 17, Max, and your dad tells me you can hold your own with anybody. And Marty, even though you're only 15, your dad says you're ready to play against adults, too."

"Ready as I'll ever be," Marty answered. "I hope there are a couple of good defencemen among all of you Mitchells. You know, to give me some protection."

The other Mitchells in the room chuckled, and Mighty Mike laughed out loud. "Don't count on it,

Marty," he said. "Look around you. You see the grey hair on some of these old farts, and the beer bellies? We need young legs on this team if we hope to win this game today."

He looked at his watch. "The good news is, we've got more fresh legs coming. The Mitchell twins from away up in Kapuskasing should be here any minute. Two big defencemen. My brother Ed is driving them down. They're smart hockey players, and both only 20 years old. Up north they call them the Kapuskasing Kids."

"We met the twins at a family reunion years ago," Max said. "We couldn't tell them apart. But it was in the summer—we've never seen them play hockey."

"They've never seen you two play either," said Mighty Mike. "It'll be fun getting acquainted with them. And I hope you'll click together on the ice. And remember, we're all getting together after the game at my place. It's just up the road in Haileybury, not far from where you used to live. There'll be more Mitchells there than you can shake a hockey stick at."

Just then, the dressing-room door flew open and two husky fellows filled the door frame. A big bear of a man slipped in behind them.

"Here they are now!" shouted Uncle Mike in greeting. "Just in time. Fellows, say hello to Bert and Barry Mitchell—the Kapuskasing Kids. And that's their dad behind them—my brother Big Ed Mitchell."

The newcomers were greeted by all their relatives and moved around the room, shaking hands and slapping backs. Max shifted along the bench to make room for the twins to sit down.

"You must be Max," Bert Mitchell said, shaking hands and flashing a wide grin. "You've really grown." He turned to Marty. "And you have too, young fellow."

The twins were identical, but Max noticed that Bert had a scar over his right eyebrow and Barry was missing a tooth. Probably from hockey injuries, he figured.

"How are your folks?" Bert Mitchell asked Max. "Does your dad still own the newspaper in Indian River?"

"Yep. Mom and Dad might get here in time for the game today. But there was a lot of snow last night back home and..."

"Dad's car isn't too good on slippery roads," Marty finished.

"So you came by train then?" Bert Mitchell asked, hauling some hockey gear out of his bag.

"Yep. We came in on the train last night," Marty said. "We wanted to get here early and visit with some of our relatives."

"We stayed with Uncle Mike and Aunt Minnie last night," Max said. "Uncle Mike's a great story-teller."

"What a smooth hockey player he was in his day," Barry said. "Did he tell you about his early years here in Cobalt?"

Marty looked up from tying a skate lace. "He did. We've heard some of his stories before, but they're still interesting. And this time Max took notes. Sometimes he writes articles for Dad's newspaper."

"What did he tell you, Max?"

Max stopped taping the blade of his stick. "He told us about coming to Cobalt on horseback in 1903, shortly after a lot of rich silver deposits were found in this area. His horse threw a shoe, so he went to a blacksmith named Fred Larose. It turned out that Larose was the man who first discovered silver up here."

Marty continued the story. "This fellow Larose was working out of a tent. And when a pesky fox stole some of his food one day, Larose threw his hammer at the little thief. He missed the fox, but his hammer struck a rock and broke part of it off. When he examined the rock, he noticed it seemed to contain some minerals. When Larose took the rock to a geologist, the fellow got all excited. The rock was loaded with copper and silver. Larose ran back to his tent and staked a claim. And he soon became a very rich man."

Max said, "When word got out, thousands of people rushed up here hoping to strike it rich. They pitched tents and built flimsy shanties anywhere they could find flat ground. And there wasn't much of that. They didn't need to dig very deep to find the silver deposits—they were everywhere. The peak year came in 1911, when 35 million ounces of silver were mined. Uncle Mike told us an ounce of silver sold for 35 cents in those days."

Bert rubbed the scar over his eye. "Did Uncle Mike get rich?" he asked.

"Rich enough, I guess," Max said. "I didn't think it would be polite to ask him. A few years ago he bought a big house up in Haileybury, about five miles north of here, right on Lake Temiskaming. We stayed there last night. And he's been very generous with his money. He's helped out his brothers and sisters, and even strangers who've fallen on hard times."

A shadow loomed over the boys. Mighty Mike had seen the cousins chatting and had crossed the room. He smiled down at them. "Are you boys gonna get dressed for hockey or are you gonna talk all day?" he asked.

"We were talking about you, Uncle Mike," Max replied. "And the stories you told us last night.

They were fascinating, especially the one about the fox and the hammer. Maybe you could tell the twins what it was like here in those days, and about some of the hockey games you played in."

Mighty Mike pulled a round watch out of his vest pocket and looked at it. "We've got a few minutes before we go on the ice," he said. "I guess there's time to tell you a couple of tales about those days. You've already told them about Fred Larose?"

Max and Marty nodded.

"Well, not long after I reached Cobalt, in the fall of 1903, the place roared to life and blossomed into a town of 10,000 people, all of them in search of the silver. A couple of my brothers came up from Ottawa and helped me stake some claims. And we did all right with those claims. We lived together in a small shack built on top of a big rock.

"Cobalt was a real boom town then. But we soon made it civilized. It wasn't long before we had the first trolley system in the North Country, with the tracks running ten miles north through Haileybury and on to New Liskeard. We had the first police detachment in the north, and the first opera house. Then, to our amazement, a rich man from Renfrew in the Ottawa Valley, a man named O'Brien, brought us a franchise in a new hockey league he'd helped organize—the National Hockey Association. Haileybury was granted a franchise, too. What a thrill it was to see all the biggest stars in hockey appear right here in Cobalt!"

Mighty Mike pointed to the far wall of the dressing room. "Look over there on the wall! Did you notice those names when you came in? You can see where Cyclone Taylor and Art Ross and Newsy Lalonde scratched their names over the bench where they sat. Why, the team owners paid those fellows small fortunes to come up here on the train and play just a game or two. I played with and against those fellows, and they were tough as a miner's boots. But the league didn't last, and neither did the boom. When the silver ran out, all the miners took off. They tried their luck someplace else."

"Why is silver so important, Uncle Mike?" Marty asked.

"Well, silver is the whitest of all the metals. It reflects 95 percent of the light that strikes it. And it conducts heat and electricity better than any other metal."

Marty was impressed. "So that's the metal we see in our knives and forks, right?"

"Not exactly," Uncle Mike explained. "The silver in cutlery can't be completely pure because it would be too soft and would bend in your hand. So it's mixed with a small amount of copper to form a silver alloy. That's called sterling silver."

"And that's what silver's mainly used for—knives and forks and spoons?" Marty asked.

"Of course not," said Uncle Mike. "It can be stretched out into fine wires. It's used in the coating of mirrors. Dentists mix it with other minerals to fill your teeth, and the photography industry uses tons of the stuff to develop pictures from your cameras."

"Don't forget coins," Max chipped in. "And silver jewellery."

"That's right, Max," Uncle Mike praised. "See, Marty, your brother's not dumb as a post—like you said he was."

"But I didn't say..." Marty began, then realized his uncle was kidding. Everybody laughed.

"Are any of those great hockey players still living up here?" Marty asked.

"No, not anymore. They all scattered. Most of them joined other pro teams. After being a boom town, Cobalt became almost a ghost town. Today the town's population is only about 1,000 people. But the big rink they built back then is still here. This is it, where we're about to play the McCoys today. Are you ready? Now let's go get 'em!"

The Mitchell brothers followed the twins across the room and out the door. They passed the wall where the names of famous pros were painted in black—men they'd only read about.

"There's Mighty Mike's name," Marty said, pointing. "Right up there with the best of them."

Their Uncle Mike laughed. "Some of those boys were mean and mercenary," he said. "They'd jump from one team to another if there was extra money in it. Sometimes the wealthiest mine owners would wager 40 or 50 thousand dollars on the outcome of a game. Fans would throw money on the ice during games—lots of money. And the players would stop to scoop it up. One big goalie, Nicholson, found a washtub somewhere and scooped up coins with his goal stick until he had a pile. Then he threw the washtub over the loot and sat on it."

The boys chuckled, imagining the scene.

"There'd be fights on the ice and fights in the stands. The miners loved to see those battles."

"I'm glad there'll be no fights today," said Max. "Just good, clean hockey—and all for fun and charity."

Mighty Mike placed a meaty hand on his shoulder. "Don't be too sure, son. Some of the McCoys can be downright mean, and they'll do anything to win. Especially Slick McCoy. Watch out for him today—he's got a shot that'll crack your head open."

Mighty Mike had some final words for the Mitchell brothers and their twin cousins before they stepped on the ice. "Speaking of all the gambling that took place years ago, I have some advice for you boys," he said, his tone serious. "All four of you might be professional players down the road—it wouldn't surprise me. And wagering on hockey games is still common in the big rinks. But none of you boys better get caught up in it, not ever. I'm tellin' you—when you get to be pros, stay away from them gamblers!"

CHAPTER 2

A SCOUT DROPS IN

Max and Marty sized up the McCoys in the pre-game warm-up. Overall, they looked to be younger than the Mitchells. And they could skate! The Mitchell brothers had expected some good-natured banter between the clubs, considering it was a family affair and a benefit game, but both teams avoided eye contact and appeared to be getting set for an all-out effort.

"Uncle Mike was right," Marty said, nudging Max. "These guys look serious."

One of the McCoy players stood out, even in the warm-up. He was a brilliant skater with a blazing shot.

"That must be Slick McCoy," Max said to Marty, before his brother stood in the net to face some warm-up shots. "Watch out that he doesn't bean you with one of those shots of his."

Marty nodded. "Uncle Mike just warned me about him again. He said Slick has a huge ego and is furious because no big-league club has ever picked him up. The word is the other McCoys had to pay him a potful of money to be here today. He said he wouldn't play with a bunch of old farts unless he got paid for it."

Just then Slick McCoy leaned into a warm-up shot that soared. It caromed off the crossbar and flew high over the wire mesh and into the stands. People scrambled to get out of the way. The puck struck an empty seat and splintered the wooden slats supporting the back.

Slick grinned and pointed a finger at the Kapuskasing Kids, as if to say, "The next shot like that will be headed straight for you two boys."

"What a show-off!" Barry snorted. "He doesn't scare me." Still, the twins began to think of how to stop McCoy.

"Don't let him loose in front of Marty's net," Bert called across to Barry as they lined up for the opening faceoff. "It looks like he knows all the tricks."

"We'll slow him up," Barry promised with a grin.

The rink was packed, even though it was just a benefit game. The fans in Cobalt loved their hockey, and the junior team they supported was on the road, with games in Haileybury and New Liskeard. And Mighty Mike Mitchell was a persuasive man. When he urged the locals to come out each year and see two determined families scrapping for a loose puck, they responded.

Even a stranger passing through town heard about the afternoon's game when he stopped in at a coffee shop. Millie Thomas, the waitress, persuaded him to buy a ticket.

"I watch a lot of hockey," the stranger told Millie, "but I can't recall ever seeing two families play against each other. I was heading on up to Haileybury to see the juniors play tonight. But I can catch a couple of periods here and still be in time to see the juniors."

Nobody in the coffee shop recognized the man. His name was Squint Walker and he was the head scout for the Toronto Maple Leafs. Walker travelled thousands of miles a year looking for raw talent. And when he found a likely prospect, he'd approach the player's parents. He'd seat them around their kitchen table and make his pitch.

"Your son has talent," he'd tell them. "In time he may become a big-leaguer with the Leafs. I'd like to have him sign a form I brought along."

"A form?"

"Yep, a hockey form. It's like a contract. It brings your son into the Maple Leaf family. And I'm willing to shell out 100 dollars to sign your boy. As I say, he's got talent."

"A hundred dollars?"

"Yep."

He'd turn to the boy. "We're willing to risk 100 bucks on you, lad. Have you ever seen so much money?"

Invariably, the youth would shake his head.

"Well, here's what 100 dollars looks like, son." Squint would show the young man a few bills, all of them fresh new ones. He'd put them on the table. Then he'd throw down a five and a ten, then a couple of twenties. The boy's eyes would begin to open wide.

"Gee, I've never seen a 20-dollar bill," the prospect would say.

Sometimes a parent would ask, "Mr. Walker, how long does this form you want my boy to sign tie him to the Leafs?"

"Why, for as long as he plays hockey," Squint would tell them. "Surely you wouldn't want him to play anywhere else. What do people in Chicago or Detroit know about hockey?"

"What about Montreal?" a father might ask. "I've always liked the Canadiens."

"A fine team," Squint would agree. "But remember, almost all of those boys are from Quebec. It would be tough for your boy to play there." He would shake his head sadly and tell a fib. "You see, nobody speaks to the English players in the Montreal dressing room. They're never made to feel welcome. Fans at the Montreal Forum curse the English players when they make the smallest mistake. It would be a horrible place for your son."

What Squint said about Montreal wasn't true. In fact, one of his finest seasons in pro hockey had been spent in a Montreal uniform. But most people accepted what the old scout told them. And then he'd speak the words that often clinched the deal.

"Think of it, folks. You'll be hearing Foster Hewitt talking about your son on the radio. Coast to coast. He'll become famous. Someday he'll be earning as much as 3,000 dollars a season. Maybe more. And you'll be able to come to Maple Leaf Gardens and see him play."

By then the parents would be convinced that their teenage son had a chance to become a hockey superstar. The boy's hand would tremble when he scribbled his name on the form. He'd scoop up the 100 bucks and shout, "Wait till the kids at school hear about this!"

Squint would beam at the parents, offer congratulations, pat the lad on the back, then tell him, "Now son, if you're going to play pro hockey, you should take out some insurance. All the top players have insurance. It just so happens that aside from my duties with the Leafs, I also represent the Great West Insurance Company. Here's another form I want you to sign. It'll protect you in case of injury or accident, on or off the ice. And I can offer you a special price for this coverage. By golly, this is your lucky day."

"How much?" the lad would ask.

"Only 100 bucks," Squint would answer. "You can give me back the money you're holding, sign this insurance form and our business is done. You'll be fully insured and on your way to stardom."

The referee dropped the puck between the sticks of Slick McCoy and Max Mitchell as the crowd applauded and the game got underway.

Slick McCoy won the draw, surprising Max with his quickness. He flipped the puck over to his left winger, broke down the ice and took a return pass. At the defence, he drilled a booming shot off the boards behind the net and darted in for the rebound, confident he could win the race for the loose puck.

But he'd never played against the Kapuskasing Kids. Bert Mitchell turned smartly and put on a burst of skating speed that startled McCoy. Bert snared the loose puck and shovelled a soft pass to his twin brother Barry, who moved it swiftly up the ice. At the Team McCoy blue line, he unleashed a heavy shot that caromed off the goal post and rolled into the corner of the rink. Max Mitchell had been following up on the play. He shifted around a defenceman and pounced on the spinning puck, then sidestepped one check and darted in front of the McCoy goal. An opposing player lunged at him and tried to smash him to the ice—Slick McCoy. But Max coolly slipped the puck between Slick's legs and, in one motion, whipped a sizzling shot high into the corner of the net. The Mitchell fans yelled with joy. Only 15 seconds played and Team Mitchell had the first goal, scored by a newcomer to the team, a good looking youth with a thatch of blond hair. The kid had displayed the poise of a veteran.

In the stands, hockey scout Squint Walker smiled. *Good goal, kid*, he thought, nodding his approval. *And those two Mitchells on defence seem to know what this game is all about, too.*

Fuming, Slick McCoy went to the bench. He took note of Max's number nine, and mumbled, "Try that between-the-legs trick again, busher, and I'll hit you so hard you'll think you fell into a silver mine."

On his next shift, Slick went all out. He displayed some clever stickhandling in the neutral zone and took two blistering shots at Marty from long range. Marty blocked them both, and made it look easy. Then Slick took off on a rink-length rush that looked promising until he reached the Team Mitchell blue line. Slick shifted, moving outside, then shifted again, changing direction. The move had paid off countless times before, when Slick cut right through the middle.

Bam!

The Kapuskasing Kids closed ranks and smashed into him, sending him reeling to the ice. He spun around like a rodeo rider tossed from a bucking bronco and landed with a crash, while the Mitchells in the crowd whooped with joy.

If Slick was hurt, Bert Mitchell didn't look back to find out. He swept up the puck and broke like lighting toward the McCoy goal. He was streaking past centre ice before Slick could even sit up. He saw a McCoy cut across the ice to intercept him and sent him reeling with a shoulder check. He swooped around a lumbering defenceman who reached out and hooked him with his stick. But Bert shook him off and faked a shot on goal. The goalie—Len "Porky" McCoy—leaped for a shot that never came. Bert zipped across the front of the net, sending slivers of snow flying four feet in the air. Then he lifted a backhander that sent the puck high into the upper corner of the net.

Mitchells 2; McCoys 0.

In the stands, Squint Walker pursed his lips and let out a piercing whistle. *What a sweet solo that was*, he thought. *That kid can motor.*

The Team McCoy coach changed lines. His players seemed a little dazed by the unexpected jolt of Bert's goal, and the new line came out determined to even the score as quickly as possible. Mighty Mike changed his line, too, and it soon became obvious the second-stringers for both clubs were far less talented than the starting combinations.

Even so, for the next few minutes, the McCoys made thrust after thrust. Their forwards buzzed around Marty Mitchell like killer bees. They soon discovered that Marty stopped everything that came into him from outside. They couldn't tell how effective he was on shots from close in, because they didn't get any. The Kapuskasing Kids wouldn't let them.

Bert and Barry stepped into the McCoy forwards with gusto. They broke up plays, rode opponents into the corners and smacked them down with bodychecks. And when a McCoy coughed up the puck, one of the Kids would go sailing off with it on an excursion down the ice.

Before the first period ended, the McCoys knew they would have to beat the toughest defence they had ever faced if they hoped to win. The two huskies patrolling the blue line knew every trick in the book.

Slick McCoy came out to play the last minute of the first period. The crushing bodycheck that had floored him still rankled. His look was grim. Nothing angers a hockey player more than being ingloriously dumped on his rear end.

Slick's stickhandling was impressive, and few defence pairs could hold him in check for long. Plenty had tried and failed, but the Kids held him at bay. Despite his frantic efforts, the McCoys were still looking for their first goal when the period ended.

The players trooped off the ice and the fans headed for the warmth of the arena lobby.

The Kapuskasing Kids were the last off the ice. In the corridor, they passed some young women in figure skating outfits waiting to go out and perform. "Are you girls going to entertain during the intermission?" Barry asked.

"Yes, we are," said a skater whose raven hair was tied with a red bow. She looked to be about the same age as the twins, and had lovely eyes.

"I wish we could stay and watch," Bert said with a smile.

After they had passed, Barry nudged his brother. "Good looking girl, Bert," he whispered. "There's something about her. She looks familiar..."

Bert gave his brother a playful shove, sending him through the dressing-room door. "Keep your mind on the hockey game," he said. "Talk to the girls later."

Squint Walker headed down the steps and thought he might take a chance on a cup of coffee. He knew from experience that most arena concession stands offered a hot liquid that barely passed for coffee, but a heaping spoonful of sugar and a generous addition of milk could often make the purchase drinkable.

He tugged at the brim of his hat and thrust his chin deep into his coat collar just as the McCoys skated through the gate leading to their dressing room. Slick McCoy looked up and caught a glimpse of Walker's face.

Holy cow! That's Squint Walker, the hockey scout, he thought to himself, astonished. *What's a big-league hockey scout doing at a nothing game in a small town like Cobalt? I wonder if somebody told him about me.*

Slick McCoy felt a surge of excitement. He convinced himself that Walker was there to look him over. *I'd better pull up my socks*, he thought. *This could be my lucky day. What if he wants to offer me a contract with the Leafs?*

It was characteristic of Slick not to tell the rest of the McCoys that Walker was at the game. If any breaks were coming as a result of Walker's visit to Cobalt, he meant to get them for himself. He was the star player on the ice, wasn't he? The most valuable? He was the only one being paid to take part. For the final two periods, he planned to really step up his pace. He'd show Walker and the entire Mitchell clan the brilliant skills he knew he had, skills he felt others never fully appreciated.

CHAPTER 3

SLICK IS SLAMMED

Marty was feeling good about his play in goal, and turned to his cousins Bert and Barry. "Want to hear a good story?" he asked.

"Sure, Marty."

"You fellows can probably tell by what you've seen of me so far is that I'm a shy kind of guy," he began. "I don't have a girlfriend like the other guys. So the other day I found a centipede crawling along the floor and I put her in a little shoebox. I said to her, 'This is your new home and you're going to be my girlfriend.' She didn't say anything, so I guess it was okay with her."

Barry said, "Is this going to be a long story, Marty?" He winked at Bert.

Marty said, "No, I'm almost finished. Anyway, I was going out to play hockey and I knocked on the door of the centipede's house and said, 'Do you want to play hockey with me?' No answer. I knocked again a little later. 'I'll ask you again. Do you want to play hockey with me?' Still no answer. I knocked a third time and said, 'Hey, do you want to play hockey or not?' She finally answered."

Marty waited, bursting to tell the punch line.

"And what did she say?" Barry asked.

Marty grinned. "She said, 'Give me a minute, will you. I'm still putting on my skates.'"

The cousins laughed out loud. "Good joke, Marty," said Bert.

"Joke?" Marty answered. "That's a true story."

When the teams skated out for the second period, the Mitchells felt optimistic about their chances of winning the 25th encounter between the Mitchells and the McCoys. As newcomers to the team, Max and Marty were pleased with their performances. Between periods, the brothers had been roundly praised for their play.

Their cousins from Kapuskasing had also been showered with compliments and were also optimistic. "The McCoys aren't so hot," Barry told Bert. "Slick's their best player."

"Don't kid yourself," Bert cautioned. "They've got a lot of fight left in them."

Although the twins looked identical and shared the same level of ability on defence, their temperaments were distinctly different. Barry was less disciplined than Bert. He was a bit reckless and willing to take chances, and he sometimes balked at taking orders from his coach. Bert was solid. He was steadier, the thinker of the two.

Behind the team bench, they could see Mighty Mike beaming at them proudly. When he caught their eye, he gave them a thumbs-up.

Right from the draw, the McCoys went on the attack, and leading the charge was Slick McCoy. The dark-haired centre had shown plenty of ability in the first period. But now, thinking he was being watched closely by a famous scout, he really exerted himself. He took three heavy shots from just inside the blue line, only to hear them thunk off Marty Mitchell's pads. Marty steered the rebounds smartly into the corner.

Slick moved the puck in closer, and a couple of thrilling skirmishes took place directly in front of Marty's goal crease. But the Kapuskasing Kids pitched in, working well together, blocking shots, deflecting pucks and dishing out a couple of thumping bodychecks.

Marty cheered them on. "Way to go, cousins! That's the way to play defence."

Slick McCoy didn't give up easily. He barrelled down the wing and scooted in on the Kids. He had swept his stick back and was ready to shoot when Barry deftly swept the puck off his blade and sent it skimming over to his brother. Bert sped toward his own blue line, spied an opening and broke past two McCoy forwards. He surged ahead and split the McCoy defence, moving right in on Porky McCoy, the opposing goaltender.

Max Mitchell had broken with Bert and hustled to catch up. He watched as Bert deked the goalie to one side, pulling him away from the post. Then he slid the puck back to Max, who fired it into the empty net.

Max threw his arms in the air and pointed at Bert. "Thanks, cousin!" he shouted over the roar of the crowd. "But you could have scored it yourself."

Bert grinned. "Maybe," he shouted back. "But they tell me you seldom miss."

The McCoys were too good to be kept off the score sheet indefinitely. Kerry McCoy, who'd played senior hockey for years, drilled a shot from the point that deflected off a teammate's stick and rolled into Marty's net.

Soon after, with Team Mitchell killing a penalty, Slick McCoy scored a goal from a wild scramble in front that brought the McCoys to within one goal of a tie.

"Watch me bust up this game now," Slick told his teammates confidently. "I've got that kid goalie figured out."

But Slick didn't bust it up. He was fast and flashy and he figured he was the one McCoy who could do it all. He began to hog the puck, ignoring his wingers. He tried to break through alone again and again, but he was stymied every time by Barry and Bert, the Kapuskasing Kids.

It began to get Slick's goat, and the Kids could tell. "We've got him fuming," Bert told his brother. "He's frustrated. Watch he doesn't lay the lumber on you. If there's a penalty coming up, let him take it. Don't retaliate."

"Yeah, sure," Barry grunted.

Bert knew his brother was unlikely to listen. He wasn't one to take punishment without giving back as much as he got.

It came on the next play. Down raced Slick, flanked by his wings. Barry was waiting, grim-faced, when Slick flashed in. When Slick darted to his left, Barry met him by the boards and slammed into him.

Crash!

Slick went sprawling. He cursed at Barry as he skidded across the ice, then scrambled to his feet. Along the boards, Slick fought with Barry for the puck. And when he failed to come up with it, he jammed the butt end of his stick deep into Barry's ribs, doubling him over.

"Why, you little rat!" Barry howled. He turned to the referee, anticipating a call, but the official had his back turned.

Meanwhile, Slick had grabbed the puck and

was zigzagging in. But he waited too long before getting his shot away. Bert Mitchell's long stick shot out and knocked the puck off his stick. It went sliding the length of the ice.

Barry edged closer to his brother. "Did you see that?" he bellowed. "The punk butt-ended me. Wait until he comes back this way. I'll get him!"

"You're up on your feet, aren't you?" Bert answered. "Can't you take it?"

"Sure I can take it," growled his brother. "But I'm not going to take it. I'll give Slick something to remember me for before this game is over."

"You stay on the ice," snapped Bert. He had always been the one with the most common sense. "Can't you see he wants you to lose your head and take a penalty or two?"

That was exactly what Slick McCoy wanted. If he could just get one of the Kids off the ice for a few minutes, he might collect a couple of goals and win the game—as well as the approval of a certain big-league scout.

The game began to get even rougher. The Kids were subjected to elbows, jabs and slashes, with Slick McCoy delivering most of them. Finally, the referee chased him to the penalty box. The Mitchell fans cheered happily.

When Slick came out for the final two minutes of the period, he was burning mad. Not only had he failed to show off his scoring skills, he had also served time in the penalty box in front of Squint Walker, the man he wanted to impress.

I've got to make up for that, he told himself. *That wasn't smart. But I've still got time to give Walker and the crowd something to talk about.*

He took the puck right off the blade of a slower teammate's stick and turned up the ice, gathering speed. At centre ice his skates were flashing. By the time he hit the Team Mitchell blue line, he was moving like an express train.

The Kapuskasing Kids were waiting for him, backing in, watching his every move.

Slick had planned to split the defence. If he could dart through in spectacular fashion, it would bring Walker and everyone else in the stands to their feet.

He hurtled toward the Kids at blinding speed, thrusting the puck ahead of him.

There was a small opening between the brothers, and he leaped toward it, soaring high off the ice.

That's when they closed the gap and sand-wiched him.

Whap!

The sound of the collision echoed throughout the arena. Slick McCoy had never been hit so hard in his life. It felt as if he had crashed into two moving oak trees. Slick spun through the air and pitched headlong over the twins' padded shoulders. They ducked as his stick windmilled high overhead. The puck was lost. A glove flew off and Slick heard himself cry "Yeeee!" before he crashed to the ice. He lay there motionless, with one arm twisted under his body.

The whistle blew.

Slick raised his head and groaned. Marty Mitchell skated out from his goal crease and nudged Slick's leg with the blade of his stick. "Are you okay, man?"

Slick groaned once more, indicating he was still alive and might live to play another day. But he was hurt, there was no question about that. All the hockey padding in the world wouldn't have protected him from that horrendous jolt.

Marty threw off his gloves and knelt beside the injured McCoy. He waved to the bench, calling for the trainer. The Kapuskasing Kids rushed over to join the players from both clubs who gathered around. Someone called for a stretcher, and Slick was eased onto it and carried off to the McCoy dressing room.

"I hope he isn't badly hurt," said Barry.

"I'm sure we hit him clean," Bert added. "No penalty was called on the play."

The referee overheard and said, "You boys hit

him clean. But Slick isn't going to believe it."

They didn't know it then, but they had just made a dangerous enemy.

CHAPTER 4

A FARCICAL ENDING

In the dressing room between the second and third periods, a doctor examined Slick McCoy. Players on both sides waited to hear what he had to say.

"He's suffered what appears to be a concussion," the doctor told the McCoys. "His right shoulder is bruised and his right wrist is definitely broken. He'll be out of hockey for several weeks."

When word of Slick's injuries reached the Kapuskasing Kids, Barry whistled. "That's too bad. I wish it hadn't happened."

Max told them they shouldn't feel that they were to blame. "I saw it from close range. It was just tough luck—it wasn't your fault."

"It's all part of the game," said Marty. "I think he twisted his arm under his body when he fell. He sure hit the ice hard!"

"Still, we feel bad," Barry said. "If he hadn't tried to leap between us..."

Bert nodded in agreement. "Honestly, I don't think it was our fault. But Slick must feel awful. He's planning a career in hockey, and he has the skills to get somewhere. This will be quite a setback."

Mighty Mike offered his opinion. "Someone told me Slick was showing off because there was a scout in the stands. And there was—my old pal Squint Walker. I also heard that the McCoys paid Slick to play in the game tonight, and that's not right—it's a benefit game, played for charity. It seems to me that Slick was putting his own self-interest ahead of everyone else's. His shoulder and wrist will heal. He'll still get a shot at pro hockey if that's what he wants. Now let's get through one more period and hope there are no more incidents."

The Mitchells faced a solemn crew of McCoys in the third period. Slick McCoy was their brightest star, and now he was gone.

When play began, Mighty Mike noticed the pace had slowed to a crawl. The McCoys were simply going through the motions. He called a timeout and huddled with Jesse McCoy, the Team McCoy manager.

"Let's put on a show for the crowd, Jesse," he suggested. "Both teams can still play to win, but let's give the crowd some entertainment. This game is supposed to be played for fun."

Jesse McCoy agreed. He laughed out loud when Mighty Mike outlined his plan.

When play began again, the McCoys tried hard to break through and score a couple of goals. But without Slick to lead them, they didn't click.

One of the McCoys—Maurice—called another timeout. He went to the bench and ladled water from a bucket into a metal cup. While he was drinking, the Kapuskasing Kids huddled along the blue line, their backs turned to Maurice. He picked up the water bucket and skated up behind the Kids, then dumped the water over their heads.

The crowd roared with laughter.

Bert laughed as he wiped water from his eyes. He immediately saw the humour in the practical joke. But Barry did not. His eyes narrowed and he started after Maurice, only to be held back by his brother.

"It's a joke, brother," Bert said, yanking on Barry's jersey. "Lighten up."

Barry relaxed. "Okay, I get it," he said. "Well, let's show the folks that we know how to joke around, too."

He went to the bench and found a couple of spare sticks, which he snapped in two with a flick of his strong wrists. He handed one to his brother and kept the other for himself. When play resumed, the twins were using the shortest hockey sticks in history, and yet they amazed the crowd with their passing and stickhandling. Up and down the ice they sped, crouched over their tiny sticks, making perfect passes to each other. But when Barry broke away and pulled the goalie, he failed to score. Why? Because during the delay at the bench, the McCoy goalie had turned his goal net around. The opening was facing the end boards.

Barry appealed to the referee in pantomime, pointing at the goalie, then pointing at the net. He pulled up his jersey and pretended to wipe tears from his eyes with his shirt.

When the referee ignored his plea for a penalty, Barry dropped to the ice on his stomach. He kicked up his heels and pounded the surface with his fists, like a spoiled brat having a temper tantrum.

The fans applauded. Laughter filled the air.

The McCoys responded with another joke. Their heaviest player, a 300-pound defenceman with a huge belly, fell to the ice, faking an injury. His teammates gathered around and the trainer rushed out, hiding something under his coat.

When his teammates moved back and the injured player arose, he was cradling a naked plastic doll to his chest. The trainer had just delivered his "baby."

From then on, the teams tried to outdo each other.

The Mitchell's trainer went to the dressing room and hammered a large nail through a puck. He inserted a skate lace through the hole and tied the puck to the blade of Max's stick. Max went out and put on a masterful display of stickhandling. The puck bobbed and bounced and never went farther than the length of the lace. He skated through and around all of the McCoys and deftly slipped the puck into the McCoy net.

But when he lifted his arms in celebration, the puck dangled from the end of his stick.

"No goal!" ruled the referee, as the crowd roared.

Maurice McCoy was back again moments later. He had been awarded a penalty shot, and all of the players gathered by the boards to watch. Maurice stepped off the bench and promptly fell down. He got up and fell again. He pretended he had never been on skates before. His legs wobbled and he skated on his ankles. His arms flailed around in the air and he rocked back and forth. He stumbled toward centre ice and nudged the puck forward. More nudges followed as he fell and got up and fell again. Laughter filled the arena. When Maurice closed in on Marty, he lunged forward and grabbed Marty around the pads, pulling him to the ice. He shoved Marty aside and then leaped to his feet, scampered after the puck and drilled it into the net like a pro.

And he finished his routine by circling the ice doing leaps and twirls like a figure skater in an ice show. The transformation from inept beginner to polished professional was astonishing, and the ovation Maurice earned lasted at least a minute.

And when Maurice took a deep bow to acknowledge the applause, his hair fell off. He'd been wearing a wig.

Oh, how the crowd laughed!

The game ended with all the players from both teams on the ice enjoying a mad scramble after the puck. Then the McCoys threw two more pucks out. Mighty Mike tossed another handful of pucks on the ice, and both goalies were peppered with shots.

Finally, the referee grew weary of the commotion and blew his whistle sharply.

"Game over!" he declared. "And it finishes in a tie—16–16. Or something close to that. Which leaves the Mitchell–McCoy series tied for another year!"

Squint Walker got up to leave. "Darnedest game I ever saw," he told the stranger next to him. "And I've seen plenty. But those two Mitchells on defence have what it takes. And the younger kids, Max and Marty, showed me a lot too."

"Too bad Slick McCoy got hurt," the stranger, a McCoy, said. "I thought he'd win the game for us. Until he went down, he was about the best player on the ice."

"Hmm," Squint Walker answered. "Maybe. But I'm not so sure."

In the Mitchell dressing room, the Kapuskasing Kids dressed hurriedly. While they threw on their street clothes, they accepted lots of praise from their teammates. Mighty Mike also made a point of telling them what a great game they'd played.

"The McCoys weren't a real test for you two," he said. "But if I know hockey, you've both got everything it takes to make it in the pros."

After they thanked him, Bert said, "We're going to the McCoy dressing room. We want to see if Slick's all right."

The McCoys looked up when Bert and Barry stood in the doorway, but Slick wasn't in the dressing room. Two or three of the McCoys came over and shook the twins' hands, and they all complimented them on their play. Then Maurice McCoy told them, "Slick's been taken to the hospital."

"I hope you know we didn't try to hurt him,"

Bert said. "We didn't throw elbows or butt ends, nothing like that."

"Yeah, we know," Maurice said. "You boys played a clean game, a great game. You're way ahead of any of us when it comes to skill. As for Slick, he can only blame himself. He took a chance trying to sail through you the way he did, and you outguessed him."

Relieved to learn the McCoys held no resentment toward them, the Kids waved goodbye and headed off to the hospital. They learned that Slick McCoy had been admitted and that Doc White was with him.

Bert and Barry waited outside the door. It finally opened, and Doc White peered at the boys over his glasses. He stepped toward them and closed the door behind him.

"I know who you are," he said. "I caught some of the game today until..." He nodded toward the door. "He's in there, but he's not very happy. And his language..."

"How is he, Doc?" Barry asked.

"It's a bad break, and he has a slight concussion, but he'll be fine."

"Can we see him for a minute?"

Doc White sighed. "Sure you can see him. But I don't think he's going to leap out of bed to embrace you."

"He probably thinks we were out to get him," said Bert.

Doc White shook his head. "I saw what happened—you sandwiched him hard. But it was Slick who tried to leap over you. And isn't that what defencemen are supposed to do?"

"It was a fair check," Bert agreed. "He walked right into it."

Doc White chuckled. "He sure did. But he seems to feel that you two deliberately crashed him to the ice, then jumped on him and tried to break his arm off at the elbow. Like I said, if you go in to see him, don't expect him to give you a hug. Maybe you'd better wait until he cools down."

Barry shook his head. "We may not get a chance to see him again. We want to say that we're sorry it happened."

"Then go ahead. But I warned you..."

Barry opened the door, and the Kids slipped into the room.

Slick McCoy was lying in bed, his right arm in a cast. The moment he saw the Kids, he snapped, "Get out!"

"Take it easy, Slick," Barry said. "If you think we deliberately tried to put you down..."

"Tried to?" Slick snarled. "Of course you tried to! And you did, just to save the Mitchells from a beating. You laid for me in a nothing game!"

"Hold on, Slick..." Bert began.

"I said, get your sorry butts out of here!" Slick interrupted. "Believe me, we'll meet again. And I'll get even!" He nodded toward his broken wrist. "I won't rest until you have one of these. You two aren't going anywhere in hockey, but I am! Or at least I was... Now you've probably ruined my career. So scram!"

He fell back on his pillow. Bert and Barry looked at each other. Bert nodded and they left the room, closing the door quietly behind them.

In the corridor, Barry said, "I didn't expect that. He's overreacting."

"He's just all worked up," replied his brother. "He'll get over it, I hope."

But the Kapuskasing Kids were soon to learn that Slick McCoy could carry a grudge as well as a hockey stick. He despised the Kids. Now he might never hear from Squint Walker—or any other scout. His hockey dreams had turned into a nightmare.

CHAPTER 5

PLANNING FOR COLLEGE

The Kapuskasing Kids caught the trolley up to Haileybury, then walked to their uncle's house. Their parents, Big Ed and Emma, had driven on ahead after dropping the twins off at the hospital.

"We might spend an hour with Slick," Barry had told them. "Go on without us. You know Uncle Mike—the family reunion will be in full swing by now."

"Besides, we've never been on a trolley," Bert added. "I can't believe they have one in the North Country."

All the lights were on in Uncle Mike's house when they arrived. They could hear fiddle music, and someone was pounding on a piano. The trolley ride had been fun, and the walk to the house took only a few minutes. The sounds of laughter and conversation could be heard from two blocks away.

"Imagine. A houseful of Mitchells," Barry had

said, starting up the walk. "I'll bet the McCoys are holding a similar gathering across town."

"If Rip Van Winkle lived in Haileybury, he'd jump out of bed and howl for silence," Barry quipped.

"Let's get a move on," urged Bert. "I want to spend some time with our cousins."

"The house will be full of cousins. And uncles and aunts as well."

"I mean our cousins from Indian River—Max and Marty. I like them. They're good kids, and good hockey players, too."

But when the Kapuskasing Kids entered the front hall and shook off their coats, they saw their father, Big Ed Mitchell, in animated conversation with a stranger.

"I can tell you you're wasting your time," they heard their father say. "The twins are going to say no." He turned and saw his sons approaching. "Here they are now. You can ask them yourself."

"What's up, Dad?" asked Bert.

"Boys, I want you to meet Squint Walker. He's a scout for the Toronto Maple Leafs."

The twins recognized the name immediately, and a thrill shot through each of them as they shook hands with the famous scout.

"We remember when you played for the Leafs," Bert said with a grin. "You led the league in scoring one year. And you were team captain for a while."

"And you've signed some of the best players in Canada for the Leafs," Barry added. "It's a pleasure to meet you, sir."

Squint Walker's handshake was firm, and his manner friendly.

"And I'm pleased to meet you," he said. "I watched you play today against the McCoys. I was impressed."

"It wasn't much of a game," Bert admitted. "The third period was a farce."

"Yes, but in the first two periods you played some sparkling hockey—both of you."

"That's high praise coming from you, Mr. Walker," Bert responded. "We didn't expect a big-league scout would be in the stands today."

"If I hadn't stopped in Cobalt for coffee, I wouldn't have been. I was on my way north to catch the junior game here in Haileybury. Then I was going to head farther north to take a look at you fellows in Kapuskasing. A waitress persuaded me to buy a ticket to the game today, since it was for a good cause. And I'm glad I did. I saw some good hockey and some bad hockey, but you fellows really stood out." He smiled at them. "And I got a bonus—a chance to see your uncle, Mighty Mike Mitchell. He was a great player in his day. And so was your dad, although he never played pro. You boys come from good stock."

Squint Walker glanced at his watch. "Boys, let me come right to the point, because I'd still like to catch the end of that junior game. How would you two like to attend the Leafs' training camp next fall?"

Before either of the twins could respond, Big Ed said, "I told you, Squint, the boys aren't interested in chasing a pro career. They're planning to go to college."

Walker chuckled and turned to the Kids. "How about speaking for yourselves?"

Bert hesitated only a moment, and then said, "Sorry, Mr. Walker, Dad's right. We're almost finished with junior hockey in Kapuskasing. Then it'll be time to buckle down and go to college."

The scout turned back to Big Ed Mitchell. "You do realize hockey has changed a lot in the past few years?"

"Has it?" asked Big Ed. "It seems to me the pro teams take the best years of a player's life and then toss him aside. And what has he got to show for it?"

"Well, he's got money."

"Not *that* much money. A young player today is just like a young player ten years ago. He'll sign with any team that asks him. What he earns in six months of hockey he blows in the other six months.

And when he's old and beaten up he has no education, nothing to fall back on. He goes into the mines or he runs a poolroom. I don't want that to happen to my boys."

"But Ed, you've worked hard to develop these sons of yours. And they've worked hard to become a pair of the best defencemen I've seen in years. Why waste all that talent?"

"I'm not stopping them," he answered. "It's their decision. Ask them again if you like."

Walker sighed. He looked directly at the twins. "So the answer is still no?" he asked.

"I'm afraid so," Barry answered. "We've talked about it often, and we've told other scouts the same thing. We want to be the first Mitchells to graduate from college."

Walker pulled on his hat and reached out his hand. "Okay, I'm convinced. But would you do me a favour? Promise you'll call me first if you ever change your minds. Some changes are coming in the organization, and I may soon be taking on a bigger job. I can tell you the Leafs will give you a better deal than you'll get with any other team."

"Sure, we can promise you that," Bert said, shaking the scout's hand once again.

"But don't wait by the phone," Big Ed cautioned him. "My boys are top students. They won't be changing their minds."

When Walker left, Big Ed threw an arm around each son's shoulders. "You know I wouldn't stand in your way if I thought a hockey career was best for you," he told them. "You kids are a step ahead of most kids in school and on the ice. But it's my job as a parent to give you the best advice I can. You know that. And I believe you'll thrive in college."

"Yep, we understand, Dad," Bert assured him. "Now we should go mingle with the rest of the family. Let's see if we can find Max and Marty in this throng."

Word quickly spread through the house that the Kids had turned down an offer to try out for the Leafs. Some of their relatives agreed with the Kids' decision, but others, like their cousin Marty, were disappointed.

"Max," he said, "you saw how good they were today. I'll bet they could make the Leafs easy. And we could have so much fun following their careers. We could take the train to Toronto and see them play."

"There's nothing wrong with getting a good education," Max responded. "And we can still have fun following their careers, Marty. They'll be stars on their college team."

"It's not the same," argued Marty. "It's not like playing for the Leafs."

The weekend passed quickly, and soon the Kapuskasing Kids were back in their hometown, playing for their junior team. Max and Marty returned to Indian River and enjoyed a successful season with their team, the Indians.

A few weeks after the hockey season ended, the Indian River Mitchells received some upsetting news. Bert Mitchell called from Kapuskasing and spoke to Max.

"My dad's in the hospital," he told his cousin. "He suffered a stroke on his way home from work yesterday—he collapsed on the front porch."

"Oh no!" said Max. "How serious is it? Is he going to be all right?"

"The doctors don't know yet. He's lost his speech and the use of his right arm. It may be weeks before he recovers enough to go back to work. Or he may never work again. Barry and I have scrapped our plans to go to college, at least for now. We were thinking we'd better take jobs in the mines."

"What does Aunt Emma say about that?"

"She hates the thought of us working underground, so she came up with a better idea. She told us to call Squint Walker and tell him about our predicament. She wants us to give pro hockey a shot."

"Won't that upset your dad?"

"Well, Mom says we won't tell him just yet. He's pretty groggy."

"Are you going to do it?"

"We just got off the phone with Mr. Walker. He's no longer chief scout for the Leafs—he's the new manager. The Leafs fired Harry Conklin, their old manager, at the end of last season."

"Really?"

"Yeah, apparently he didn't get along with the Leafs' coach and made all kinds of bad decisions. Mr. Walker wants Barry and me to come Toronto, to training camp. And he said he'd advance us some money to help pay for Dad's hospital bills."

CHAPTER 6
AT TRAINING CAMP

Early in September, the Kapuskasing Kids boarded the overnight train bound for Toronto, en route to the Leafs' training camp. Their father was making a slow but steady recovery—his speech was still slurred and he was still a bit confused, but he was in good hands. Even so, they were reluctant to leave their mother, but she insisted they go.

"This is a big opportunity for you boys," she told them when she helped them pack their bags. "I want you to make the most of it. I'll be just fine."

She pulled Bert aside and spoke to him privately. "Son, I want you to keep an eye on your brother. Sometimes Barry can be a bit headstrong. He'll want to do things his own way. There are lots of temptations in the big city, and I worry that he might lose control of himself. You've always been the one to use good old common sense. So please look after your brother."

At the train station she offered a few more

words of advice. "Big Ed taught you all he knows about hockey, and his lessons should serve you well. Just remember, hockey's a business for you now, a serious business. There's big money involved—you won't be playing for fun anymore. So attend to business."

When the train left the station, tears welled up her eyes. She wondered when she would see her sons again. She could no longer think of them as her boys, since they were almost grown men, off to the hockey wars. And she worried about their future.

When they arrived in Toronto, the Kids went straight to Maple Leaf Gardens. They stopped at rinkside and gazed in awe at the gleaming ice surface, the brightly painted seats and the famous gondola high over their heads where broadcaster Foster Hewitt thrilled millions every Saturday night with his play-by-play descriptions of Leaf games.

An usher dressed in a blue uniform walked toward them. "I can always tell first-timers to the Gardens," he said with a smile. "They don't speak, but their mouths are wide open."

The twins blushed. "I guess our jaws did drop at the sight of this place," Bert admitted. "It's ten times the size of our rink back home."

"I was one of the construction workers hired to build the Gardens," the usher told them. "That was back in '31. We got it built in record time—six months. And at a cost of only 1.5 million dollars. Some of us took stock in the building in place of payment. It'll be worth a bundle some day in the future."

"It must be the biggest and best hockey rink in the world," Barry said, his eyes still wide.

"Maybe not the biggest," the usher replied, "but those of us who work here think it's the best. And it's not just for hockey. We've had professional lacrosse games here, indoor softball, political rallies, religious services and even dog racing."

"Dog racing?" Max asked.

"Sure. But not for long. One night the mechanical rabbit the dogs chase around the track broke down. And you can't hold a dog race without a rabbit. All the dogs stopped running and wandered off somewhere. As far as I know they went looking for fire hydrants." He laughed at his little joke.

"Say, can you tell us how to get to the team offices?" Bert said. "We're here to see Mr. Walker."

"I'll do better than that—I'll take you there myself. You boys must be hockey players."

"That's right. We've been invited to try out with the Leafs," Barry said proudly as the twins followed the usher up a flight of stairs.

The old fellow wasn't impressed. "I've seen lots of young fellows like you come here to try out," he told them, "and I haven't seen too many who catch on. Only the best play for the Leafs. Not too many lads make it."

Barry bristled. "Well, we plan to," he said confidently.

When the twins entered the team offices, they received a hearty welcome from Squint Walker, the Leafs' new manager. Squint had grown tired of the tricky tactics he had to use as a scout, and welcomed his new job, where he could be straightforward and honest with his players.

"Fellows, I took on this new job on the condition that I be given a free hand. I told Mr. Smythe, the team owner, that I wanted a young team, a team that never quits. I'm hoping you two boys can be a big part of the Leafs' future. But you must realize that it's a big jump from the amateurs to the pros."

"All we're asking for is a chance," Barry said. "If we don't make it..."

"I'm betting you'll make it, but maybe not right off the bat. You may have to spend some time with one of our minor-league teams for seasoning. Understood?"

"We understand."

He gripped each of the twins by the hand. "Then

welcome to the Toronto organization. My secretary has booked you a hotel room for the night. Tomorrow we open training camp."

The Leaf training camp was held in St. Catharines, Ontario, a two-hour bus ride from Maple Leaf Gardens.

After a few days of conditioning drills on and off the ice, and after a few of the obvious misfits and less talented players were sent home, the team played a Blue and White game.

The old rink echoed with the thud of puck against boards, the clash of sticks, the hoarse shouts of players all hoping to win a position in the organization and the paycheque that went with it.

The Kapuskasing Kids were assigned to the White team, and the action was extremely fast, much faster than junior hockey. On the twins' first shift together, Drillon, a ten-year veteran of the Leafs, moved in on the Kids, shifted into the clear and unleashed a shot. Bert Mitchell leaped in front of it, hoping to block it, but the puck zipped under his body and struck the goalie's pads. It bounced in front, and Barry went for the rebound. He snared it, but hesitated a fraction of a second before clearing, and the delay proved to be costly. Drillon stole the puck off his stick, wheeled and fired the puck into the corner of the net.

"You've got to be quicker than that, rookie," Drillon laughed as he skated away. "This is the NHL."

Midway through the period, Drillon was parked in front of the net again. A loose puck bounced toward his stick, and he reached for it. Suddenly he went sprawling on the seat of his pants, landing hard. Barry had come from nowhere and had flattened him. "That quick enough for you?" Barry asked, before racing away with the puck and taking a hard shot at the Blues' goalie. The puck bounced off his blocker and sailed high into the stands.

There was a whistle and a line change. The Kids sank onto the bench and reached for towels. They steamed sweat and their muscles ached. It was only 11 in the morning, but it seemed like they'd been on the ice all day. This was a big-league training camp. They'd assumed it would be tough, and they were right. "But not this tough," groaned Barry.

The Whites edged the Blues 4–3, and each of the twins earned an assist.

"We may be back in Kapuskasing before we know it," grunted Bert when he emerged from his shower. "Or in the minors. These guys are hockey players."

"We're as good as any of them," Barry snorted. "Did you see me put Drillon on his back? And he's been a star for years."

A week later, they were still in camp.

They were somewhat surprised to have survived. Two prospects from Winnipeg who'd shown up thinking that a training camp would be full of fun were no longer around. And some of the veterans quickly realized that Squint Walker meant business. When he said he planned to shake up the club, he meant it. Contracts or no contracts, whether you were a proven star or a potential headliner, nobody's job was safe. Squint made that perfectly clear.

When a 20-goal scorer from the previous year's team reported a week late, with a beer belly hanging over his belt, Walker made a phone call to Detroit.

"You've been traded to the Red Wings," he told the astonished forward. "They may tolerate beer guzzlers, but we won't. Goodbye and good luck to you."

Squint had delivered a message. He would not accept players who didn't have the proper attitude. The veterans in camp buckled down and nervously watched the rookies, eager young fellows who had never made it to a big-league training camp before. Nothing was certain.

Most of the rookies didn't last long. In the second week, some were handed tickets to the minors, while others simply disappeared. But the ones who remained, like the Kapuskasing Kids, stayed hopeful.

The Leafs' head coach, the legendary Dick Irvin, had little to say to the boys from the North Country. If they impressed him, they never heard about it. But he watched them more closely than they realized. They weren't aware that Irvin had talked to his favourite defenceman, Bob Goldham, and asked him to take them under his wing.

Goldham showed them how to finish off plays, how to protect the goalie without blocking his view and how to get the puck out of the defensive zone quickly. They learned fast, and in a matter of days Goldham told them, "There's not much more I can teach you boys."

Now, in another Blue versus White scrimmage, they were strutting their stuff in what was close to regular-season conditions.

"Out you go," Irvin snapped at them.

The Kids leaped over the boards.

The Blues came flying in on the attack. The puck carrier sped past mid ice and brought the puck over the blue line, attempting to swoop around Bert. But Bert jostled him, then lashed out with his stick and knocked the puck over to his brother. Barry scooped it up, sidestepped an advancing wing and quickly flipped the disc to one of his own forwards, who took a high, hard shot on goal.

"Nice play, boys," shouted Buddy Broda, the goalie.

Moments later, the Blues came in again. This time Barry rode the incoming centre into the boards inside the blue line. The puck skimmed out, and Bert snapped it up. He cut up centre and fed a sharp pass to his right winger. A return pass hit the blade of his stick, and he barrelled through the opposing defence, knocking one man down and shifting around another.

He was in the clear! The goalie hugged the post, leaving the entire right side of the net open, hoping to tempt Bert into the obvious shot. When Bert faked his shot to the open space, the goalie moved quickly to cover it. Bert waited a split second for him to leave the post, then slipped the puck into the open corner.

He was exultant as he skated back and tapped gloves with his right winger, the set-up man. "Nice pass," he said, smiling. He felt a great thrill in knowing he could beat a big-time defence and an NHL goalie on what was almost a solo rush.

The Kids were sitting on the bench when they noticed that the Blues had sent out a new man at centre. Before the puck was dropped, Bert turned to Barry and said, "That guy looks familiar."

"He should," replied Barry. "That's Slick McCoy."

"McCoy! Where did he come from?"

A teammate sitting next to them overheard. "It's McCoy all right. He reported late because he had to get treatment on his wrist and elbow. He told me that some busher in a nothing game deliberately smashed him on the wrist. Squint wants to find out if he still has his booming shot."

"Okay, boys, get back out there," the coach ordered, tapping the Kids on the back. "Only a few seconds left."

Slick McCoy won the draw and broke toward the Kids. He was smooth and tricky but not in game shape, and Bert knocked the puck off his stick. Slick's right winger picked it up and fed Slick a pass. He moved in from a sharp angle, tried to come in front and ran smack into Barry. The collision sent Slick spinning around, and the puck came loose. Barry hoisted it down the ice just as the whistle blew to end the game.

Barry stood over Slick as he stumbled to his feet. "Hi, Slick," he said amiably. "How are you doing?"

Slick glared at him, unsmiling. His eyes blazed. He muttered something under his breath and skated away.

Barry looked blankly at the retreating player. It wasn't in his nature to hold grudges or malice toward others, and he couldn't understand it when others didn't behave the same way.

"What was that all about?" asked Bert. "What did he say?"

"Something about kissing. Kiss my... something..." Barry replied. "I didn't catch it all."

"Oh, it's going to be fun around here if he makes the club," Bert predicted.

CHAPTER 7

DEALING WITH A PUCK HOG

The boys called home that night. "How's Dad?" Bert asked his mom.

"He's coming along. He'll be home from the hospital in a few days, but it may be a long time before he recovers the use of his arm. If ever. He's got some of his speech back, though. He was asking about you two again today."

"You told him where we are?"

"I had to. He knew you hadn't been in to see him and wanted to know how I was managing with you boys away at college. I couldn't lie to him, so I told him about our decision."

"How did he take it?"

"He grumbled a little. And he sighed and said it was probably all for the best. He said to tell you he'll be rooting for you to make it with the Leafs. Do you think you will?"

"Barry thinks we're a cinch to make it, but I'm not so sure. The coach and Squint Walker will be making their final cuts tomorrow. We'll call you back tomorrow night."

There was extra tension in the dressing rooms the following morning. The moment of truth was at hand. Only about 30 players remained in camp, and following the morning scrimmage another ten would get their release or a trip to the minors.

Slick McCoy had refused to exchange even a nod with the Kids, but he'd befriended a player named Cuddles Kramer, a hulking defenceman who excelled at hockey's dirty tricks. Kramer had earned his nickname for his tendency to use his powerful arms to hold players up against the boards, attempting to crush their ribs. Like McCoy, Kramer looked on the Kids with disdain. He'd hacked and grabbed and cursed at them since the first day on the ice.

"If he doesn't leave me alone, I'm going to pummel the guy," Barry threatened.

"Stay away from him," said Bert. "He's desperate, afraid he won't make the team. And I'm sure Slick is encouraging him to stick it to us because of his brute strength."

As for McCoy, he had worked hard to impress the coach and the manager. The reporters from all the newspapers wrote glowingly of his stickhandling and passing skills.

Once he gets his shot back, he'll be a leading scorer for the Leafs, wrote one. The reporter asked Coach Irvin if he agreed with that assessment, and Irvin replied with a terse, "We'll see."

The veterans on the club had their own opinions that they exchanged only among themselves. They agreed that Slick was an outstanding skater and stickhandler. But most of his shots were soft, fluttering through the air like a butterfly.

Buddy Broda, the Leafs' number-one goalie, snickered. "I only wish all the other guys in the league had shots like that. I'd get a record number of shutouts this season."

The Kapuskasing Kids, with the experienced Broda tending goal in back of them, pitched into their final scrimmage of training camp with enthusiasm. Coach Irvin had experimented with other defence combinations and had even played the Kids with other partners—but not for long. He always came back to using them as a duo. It became clear that if one made the club the other would be signed as a matter of course.

Slick McCoy was at his best during the scrimmage. On flashing blades, he stickhandled with great dexterity, ragging the puck, then darting in. And he earned a big cheer from the railbirds when he scored a goal on Broda, tapping in a rebound.

"I'm glad we weren't on the ice for that one,"

Bert said to Barry as the coach called for a line change.

Slick stayed out on the ice, grinning now, happy to have scored.

Moments later, he wound up behind his net and embarked on a dazzling rush. He raced in, his left winger open. He faked a pass at the blue line, then shifted over the line.

The Kids didn't budge. They waited for his next move.

McCoy swung wide and tried to scurry around Bert, but he was immediately ridden off to the side and slammed into the boards. He kicked the puck with his skate in an effort to get it to a line-mate, but Bert's stick lashed out and trapped it. Bert slipped it swiftly ahead to Terry Noble, his centreman, and Noble whirled around and dashed in on the opposing netminder, scoring easily.

Noble had thrown his hands in the air to celebrate his goal when he was cruelly blindsided by Cuddles Kramer. Kramer gave Noble an elbow to the face and a cross-check to the side of the head. Noble went down and stayed down.

Before Kramer could turn away, Barry streaked in, dropped his gloves and walloped him. "What a dirty check!" he screamed at Kramer. He peppered Kramer with a flurry of punches until the big defenceman staggered and fell.

"Nobody hits a teammate of mine like that," Barry snarled, leaning over the dazed defenceman.

Bert and several other Blues dashed in and pulled Barry away from the bloodied Kramer, who held a hand to his bleeding mouth.

During a break in the play, Bert sidled up to his brother. "Remember what dad told us: Don't go starting fights, but be prepared to defend yourself when one breaks out. I think you started that one with Kramer."

"Well, he deserved it," Barry muttered. "He's a goon."

"Still, we haven't made the team yet. Coach might not like it if we show him we're hot-tempered."

Bert didn't have to worry about the coach's reaction. Behind the bench, Squirt Walker nudged Dick Irvin. "Did you see Barry Mitchell barrel into Kramer? I love the way he came to Noble's rescue."

"Kramer's a goofball, a thug on skates," Irvin replied. "The kid showed me he's got spunk."

The scrimmage continued and the Kids teamed up for some impressive defensive plays. Twice they trapped McCoy trying to squeeze between them and sent him spinning. McCoy broke his stick on the ice in frustration.

Before the scrimmage ground to a halt, Squint Walker approached Coach Irvin. "Those kids are mighty hard to beat. McCoy can't get around them."

"Maybe he's trying too hard," replied the coach. "Trying to do everything himself. For a few seconds he looks like a million dollars out there. But when he does break through, his shot drifts through the air like he's playing horseshoes."

"I guess it's that broken wrist he suffered. Maybe it didn't set right," Walker said.

"Probably. It looks like he's being careful— hesitating that split second before he lets the shot go. He who hesitates in this league is lost. They don't give you any split seconds."

"Maybe the wrist will come around. Maybe he'll get over it. After all, he's always been a top goal scorer on other teams he's played with."

"We can't risk it," Irvin replied. "Last year's goals aren't going to help us this season. No, I don't think we should keep him. Besides, he's too much of a puck hog, never using his wingers enough. He's accustomed to doing most of the scoring himself. Now that his arm is bad, he's out of luck."

"I guess you're right, Coach. Besides, his attitude is sure to be a problem if we sign him. He can't even get along with the two new kids on defence."

Just then, Slick McCoy was winding up for another rush. He'd seen the coach and the manager shake their heads after his last shot on goal, a looping drive that Broda had snatched out of the air with his glove. He knew what it meant. His hockey future was not going to be in Toronto.

Slick was angry and bitter. He knew the Kapuskasing Kids were to blame. They had ruined his once-promising career. His right arm was not what it had been, and his once-deadly shot had lost its punch. He might well be headed for hockey's scrap heap.

He flashed across the blue line and burst in against the defence, determined to knock one of the Kids bowlegged. All week he had held his temper in check, but it didn't matter anymore. He swung around, gripped his stick in both hands and cross-checked Barry Mitchell across the head and shoulders.

Barry crashed to the ice, stunned. He was bleeding from the nose. Bert dropped his stick and gloves and laced into McCoy. When anybody dared belt one Kid, he'd better look out for the other.

Bert took a wild swing and pasted Slick in the eye. Slick howled and threw a return punch that caught Bert on the jaw and almost knocked him down. Bert shook his head and came back in with both fists flying.

Bap-bap-bap!

Slick's head snapped back as the short punches caught him in the face. He tried to cover up, but Bert nailed him with three more punches before he sank to the ice.

Slick turned on his stomach and covered his head with his arms. "Why, you... you... turtle!" Bert shouted at him in frustration. "Stand up and fight!"

By then Barry was up on his skates and tugging on Bert's jersey, holding his brother away. Other players pitched in as peacemakers and within seconds the battle was over.

Bert was still fuming when he looked at his brother. Barry was laughing.

"What's so funny?" growled Bert.

Barry chuckled. "What was that you were telling me—don't go starting fights? Or something like that."

"Yeah, well, sometimes you can't help but get involved. And it's lucky for you I did. Slick might have killed you."

That's when Coach Irvin called Slick McCoy to the bench. "That was a dirty hit against Barry Mitchell," he told him.

"He deserved it," Slick snarled, still angry. "I'm not sorry. He broke my wrist last winter."

Irvin thumbed Slick to the dressing room. "Get dressed. You're finished here."

Slick exploded. "Oh, yeah? Well, that suits me. Maybe I'm through with your lousy team, but I'm not through with hockey. And I'm not through with those punk kids you've got on defence. I'm telling you, you'll all see a lot more of me before this season is over!"

"Beat it, Slick!' ordered the coach.

Slick McCoy beat it. And when he left camp that morning, Kramer went with him.

The Kapuskasing Kids, having retrieved their sticks and gloves, witnessed the exchange between Slick McCoy and Irvin, then drew a sigh of relief. Two enemies gone in the blink of an eye. They thought they had seen the last of Slick McCoy.

They were wrong.

CHAPTER 8

THE SEASON OPENS

Opening night of the hockey season at Maple Leaf Gardens! The capacity crowd was full of sports-writers and celebrities, with men in top hats and tuxedos and bejewelled women in long gowns and fur wraps. Scottish pipers marched across the gleaming ice.

Following the warm-up, men in blue and white cardigans wheeled water-filled barrels around and around the rink's frozen surface, making fresh ice. A few inches below their feet, under the artificial ice and below the cement floor of the arena, several miles of brine-filled copper pipes lay side by side. The frigid brine chilled the floor and quickly froze the new water that spilled from the barrels.

In the midst of it all, drinking everything in, were the Kapuskasing Kids, the Maple Leafs' most talked about rookie defence pair in years.

Life in the big city is enough to put any rookie

off balance. But when the two in the spotlight have been yanked from the obscurity of a small mining town in the North Country to the hub of the hockey world, they need plenty of common sense, maturity and guidance if they hope to keep their feet on the ground.

Bert Mitchell took it all in stride. The Leafs were a major-league team in a thriving metropolis, but hockey was still hockey. Toronto was much bigger than Kapuskasing, but the ice was the same size. And the fans, while there were more of them, didn't hoot and holler any louder. It wasn't easy to throw Bert off his stride.

His twin brother was different. He enjoyed the bright lights of the city and the hangers-on who made a big fuss over him and wanted to show him around. But Bert's sane attitude had a steadying influence on Barry.

"Take it easy," advised Bert. "Don't be tempted. We're here to play hockey. This is how we make our living now."

So they stuck to a schedule and trained faithfully.

Squint Walker and Coach Irvin expected big things from them in the home opener against the Chicago Black Hawks, a powerful team with Stanley Cup aspirations. Barry had a bad attack of stage fright when he saw the huge crowd, and he was positively gaping and quaking during the impressive opening ceremonies.

Coach Irvin wisely started a veteran duo on defence. Cleary and Richards were on the blue line when the puck was dropped.

On the players' bench, Bert nudged his brother and tried to calm him down. "There's a huge crowd and the hockey is faster, but what of it? We're better players than we were last season. We can keep pace with these guys."

Barry wasn't so sure. "I hope you're right," he mumbled, his eyes scanning the crowd.

In the opening minutes, the Leafs cut loose with a series of rapid-fire attacks on the Chicago defence. Bert and Barry forgot about the crowd, although the cheering was deafening. They were sent over the boards when the starters changed on the fly, and it was all done so quickly and with so little fuss that they were in the thick of the game before they had time to realize it.

Chicago's second line slipped over the boards at the same time, and soon the visitors were making things so hot for the Kids that they had no time to think about stage fright or anything else.

Three determined forwards in black, white and red jerseys circled inside the Toronto blue line, buzzing around, each of them striving to become the first goal scorer of the new season. Pappin, left winger on the line, streaked in from the side. He was fast and shifty but not quite shifty enough when he tried to step around Bert and go in for a shot on goal. Bert stepped into him so hard that Pappin crashed to the ice. It brought the Gardens' crowd to its feet. Thrilled by the ovation, Bert snapped up the puck just as the Chicago centreman made a dive for it. Bert flipped the puck smartly over the centre's outstretched stick to Lewicki, a waiting winger, who raced away with it and almost scored on Hall, Chicago's all-star netminder.

Back came the Hawks. Mosienko, one of the fleetest players in the game, emerged from a scramble with the puck on his stick and left his check flat-footed. He was skating full tilt when he crossed the Toronto blue line and moved wide to go around Barry. But Barry could skate fast, too, and he rode Mosienko into the corner, pestering him, shoving him and finally claiming the puck from him and taking it to safety behind the net.

Then Barry saw open ice ahead and took off. He roared down the rink and sent Pappin spinning with a shoulder check as he laid a perfect pass over to Burgess on right wing. Burgess returned the pass as Barry hit the Chicago defence and decided to barrel straight through.

But Moose Moran was there to greet him, and

Moran was a rock. He set himself to give this brash rookie the works. When Moran plastered an opponent, he usually stayed plastered.

Thunk!

Barry was rocked but barely slowed down. He had seen the check coming and slid off at an angle, leaving Moose Moran frustrated and thinking to himself, *That kid should be flat on the ice, crying for his momma.* Meanwhile, Barry danced inside, settled the bouncing puck on the blade of his stick, then rifled a shot at Hall from ten feet out. He streaked past the net and piled with a crash into the end boards. He didn't need the roof-raising roar of the crowd to tell him he had scored. He knew the puck was ticketed for the upper corner of the net the instant he let it go.

Leaf fans were still cheering when Barry skated back to his position, a big grin on his face. He had won them over in an instant. They applauded the good looking youngster who proved he could dish it out on the defence and skate like blazes on the attack. He'd scored the first goal of the game, the first goal of the new season. And he was playing in his first NHL game.

"Way to go, brother!" Bert shouted when Barry ranged alongside. "A beauty."

The Kapuskasing Kids spent a few moments on the bench before the lines were changed again.

The Black Hawks sent out their top scorers—
Mosienko and the Bentley brothers, Max and
Doug. It was one of the most feared lines in hockey.
A Chicago newspaperman had dubbed them the
Pony Line, because they were small but high-
spirited and galloped around the ice like wild
horses. Coach Irvin sent the Kids out to corral
them, along with his checking line.

Max Bentley dipsy-doodled down the ice with
his linemates keeping pace. He shook off a check
and skimmed a pass across to Mosienko.
Mosienko tried to swing around Bert, found it
couldn't be done and turned back. He drifted a
pass across to Doug Bentley, who dropped it
between his legs to his brother Max. The clever
playmaker no sooner had the puck on his stick
when he was stopped in his tracks by what felt
like a small earthquake. Bert Mitchell stepped
into him and sent him tumbling, to the delight of
the Toronto crowd.

Bentley climbed slowly to his feet, tried gamely
to carry on, then signalled to the bench for a
replacement.

The Kapuskasing Kids had broken in with a
bang!

The Black Hawks redoubled their efforts.
Occasionally, a lone puck carrier broke through
for a shot on goal. But he had to hurry his shot

because one of the Kids was usually right on his heels.

Broda, the Leaf goalie, slapped his stick on the ice in appreciation. He was well protected. By the time the first period ended, the Black Hawks realized that the Kapuskasing Kids spelled poison to opposing forwards. And when the Kids skated off, it was to a spontaneous wave of handclapping.

"If only Dad could be here to see us," said Bert.

The Black Hawks managed a goal in the second period, when the Leafs, playing shorthanded, allowed Bentley to work in close and slam the puck past Broda. But the home team fought back a few minutes later, with Terry Noble scoring to put the Leafs in front again. Noble scored again on the same shift, clicking with a long shot that caromed off the crossbar and into the net.

Down by two goals at the start of the third period, the Black Hawks had to open up. The Bentleys and Mosienko went on a goal hunt with a vengeance. Mosienko drove a long shot off the boards behind the Leaf goal and the trio raced in after it.

For the next few minutes, the Kids thought it was raining hockey pucks. A Leaf forward was given the gate for tripping, and the Hawks had the man advantage. They swarmed around Broda's net, shooting from all angles. It was a sustained ganging attack that had the crowd on its feet, oohing and aahing and shouting themselves hoarse.

At least three times the Kids swept the puck out of danger, skimming it the length of the ice with Broda sprawled in his net. They intercepted passes in the goalmouth, blocked shots and dished out thumping bodychecks. When they sent the puck skipping down the ice, the Hawks scurried after it and came flying back.

The Bentleys and Mosienko were established goal scorers, accustomed to success. But on this night, apart from the one goal, they were denied. Broda stopped everything that got through and the Kids made sure he got maximum protection.

Finally, Barry intercepted an ill-timed pass and broke away, surging free of a milling group of players. He scooted out over the blue line, the puck glued to his stick. Andy Blair, a Leaf winger, broke with him while the Hawk forwards wheeled and took off in pursuit.

Barry had only one man to beat in front of the Chicago goal. He zoomed in on the luckless defender, weaving and swerving, then laid a perfect pass over to Blair. Blair let drive from 30 feet but Hall, the Chicago goalie, took it on his chest, tried to smother the puck and missed. It rolled out in front as Barry drove in.

He faked a shot as the goalie went to his knees. Barry poked the puck over to Blair as he swerved to avoid the goal post, and the Leaf forward connected on his second chance. Blair drilled the puck over the prostrate netminder. The red light blinked. The fans went wild. It was a wonderful display of teamwork, and it took some of the sting out of the Hawks' attack.

The game finished with the Hawks trailing by three goals, and the Kapuskasing Kids were the talk of the town.

"Dynamite on Ice" wrote one of the leading sportswriters in the *Globe and Mail* on the following day: *Bert and Barry Mitchell, already known as the Kapuskasing Kids, stole the show at last night's NHL opener between the Leafs and the Black Hawks. They had Leaf fans roaring in delight after they bumped and skated the Hawks into submission. New manager Squint Walker looks like a genius for persuading them to sign big-league contracts. While Bert Mitchell was a standout defensively, his twin brother Barry was the offensive star, scoring one goal and setting Blair up for another. They were dynamite on ice.*

Barry found a pair of scissors and began cutting out the clipping. "I think I'll start a scrapbook," he said, grinning.

Bert frowned. "Don't be getting a swelled head

just because you got your name in the paper."

"Who said I had a swelled head?"

"Nobody. But don't get one."

"Don't worry about me. But it's pretty obvious we're going to be big stars in this league. The Leafs might not have won last night without us."

Bert's advice to his brother was much the same as their dad's advice when they called home. In a weak voice, he told them, "Your mother and I listened to the game on the radio. Congratulations—you're off to a great start. But remember that it's just one game. Don't be getting any fancy ideas that you're the best thing to come along since the forward pass. I want both of you to keep your feet on the ground."

The twins promised they would. Then Bert had the final word. "By the way, Dad. We were over at the University of Toronto today. They have summer classes, and they told us we could register to take some courses in the off-season. It may take a few years, but we can still get our university degrees."

"That's the best news you could have told me," their father said.

CHAPTER 9

BARRY'S BAD COMPANIONS

When the Leafs fired manager Harry Conklin and replaced him with Squint Walker prior to the season, Conklin did not stay unemployed for long. His old friend Joe Norris, owner of the Detroit Red Wings, was looking for a new man at the helm. His Red Wings were floundering, and he offered Conklin the job of manager.

"But it's a one-year deal," he told Conklin. "Friend or not, if you don't build me a winner, you'll be gone."

When Conklin accepted, he told his boss he had one burning ambition. "I want to show the Leafs they made a big mistake in letting me go because of that stupid coach, Irvin," he said. "I want to beat that club more than any other in the league."

Then he began looking for new talent. When he heard that the Leafs had dropped Slick McCoy, he gambled by offering Slick a contract.

"But the guy has lost his shot," his scouts told

him. "He can skate like the wind, but his shot wouldn't break a milk bottle."

"It's because he broke his wrist," said Conklin. "I know a guy, Bonesetter Bailey, who thinks he can do something."

"If he can't do it, nobody can," said the scouts. "Good thinking, Harry."

"It's not going to cost us much to find out. Slick is desperate for an NHL career. He'll sign for next to nothing, and if we get him back in harness, we'll have one of the best centres in the league."

Bonesetter Bailey was a sleepy-eyed little man who'd dropped out of medical school because of financial problems. He trained athletes and specialized in treating the injuries to which hockey, football and baseball players are prone. One ball player, a pitcher, claimed that Bonesetter had cured him of a "dead arm" and credited him with the 20 wins he'd produced for the Detroit Tigers. Ligaments, tendons, muscles, bones—what the Bonesetter didn't know about his chosen field wasn't worth knowing.

When Slick McCoy reported to the Red Wings, he went straight to the Bonesetter, who examined his injured arm and had the team doctor take x-rays. Both men studied them carefully.

"It looks like you came back too soon after the initial break," Bonesetter Bailey told Slick. "You hockey players are always so anxious to get back in the game. I'm going to give you an exercise program I want you to follow. You can skate, but you can't play."

"We won't put you in a game until the Bonesetter gives the word," Conklin told Slick. "You'll stay in shape, but no scrimmages and no shooting drills. Don't put any strain on that arm. Do exactly what the Bonesetter tells you."

Slick McCoy nodded. "That's fine with me. I'll do anything to get my shot back."

"By the way," Conklin said. "I hear you didn't get along with those two whiz kids the Leafs signed, the ones they call the Kapuskasing Kids."

"There's no reason why I should," Slick growled. "They're the ones who broke my wrist and tried to cost me my career. I can't wait to get back into the game and rip through them for some goals."

"I know the feeling," Conklin said. "There's no team I'd rather beat than the Leafs. They gave me a raw deal. So we have something in common. Now how about those kids—do they have any weaknesses?"

"Not really," admitted Slick. "They're both big and strong. They learned their hockey from their dad, Big Ed Mitchell. The thing is, they've always played together. Each one knows what the other is going to do."

"So no weaknesses then?"

Slick saw that Conklin would be a more useful ally than the thug Kramer in his quest to get even with Bert and Barry Mitchell. He thought hard and eventually said, "Well, they're different even though they're twins. Bert is a straight-up guy. Very level-headed. You can't shake him. But the other twin—Barry—is different. He enjoys the limelight. If anybody is going to have his head turned by all the attention a pro player gets, it'll be Barry. He's lived in a small town all his life. Never experienced life in the city."

"And all the fun that can mean?"

"Right. He's like a kid in a candy store. He wants to sample everything."

"Hmm. I've seen that happen. Years ago I signed me a left winger who had it all. Man, was he good! But when he reached the NHL he flouted all the rules and got to drinking and carousing. In two years he was finished—on the skids."

"I wouldn't say that's going to happen to Barry Mitchell," Slick said. "But it could. And if he starts living the Hollywood lifestyle and becomes a party guy, the Leafs' defence could be in trouble."

"Thanks for the information, Slick," said Conklin. "I know a guy who knows the Toronto scene. I'll see if he can find someone who can get to Barry Mitchell, show him a really good time and put him in a party mood. I'd be willing to pay a few bucks to someone who could start the rookie on a downhill slide. Maybe I'll introduce you to my friend, too—he's helped out lots of young players."

Slick grinned, "That sounds like a great plan."

"Meanwhile, you do what the Bonesetter tells you," said Conklin. "I'm betting he'll help you get your shot back. You'll soon be back in the league making big bucks and I'll look like a genius."

"And the Leafs will be wishing they'd never let either one of us go," Slick said with a laugh.

Slick didn't see any action for the first month of the new season, but his wrist was beginning to respond to the Bonesetter's ministrations and he hoped that it would soon regain its old strength and flexibility. From the press box, Slick fumed as he watched the Leafs pound the Wings 5–1 in the first game between the long-time rivals.

Their first swing around the league established Toronto as the top team in the six-city circuit. Fans and commentators were already touting the Kapuskasing Kids as the top defence pair in the league, and all agreed that they were going to be around for a long time. They had dash and youth. They could move the puck out of the zone and neutralize all but the best of forwards when the puck was inside their own blue line. And when the Leafs were pressured or killing a penalty, there was always a chance that one of the Kids would grab a loose puck and barrel down the ice, either assisting on or scoring a goal.

One veteran sports columnist wrote regularly about the Kids: *The boys still have a few things to learn, but not many. I predict all-star berths for the two of them, maybe not this year, but soon. And what a tough choice it's going to be for those of us charged with selecting the rookie of the year. There's only one trophy, but there are two Mitchells. And it's just got to be one of them—but which one? I might have to flip a coin to determine my vote.*

Barry chuckled when he read that and reached for the scissors. "Another item for my scrapbook," he told Bert. "The pages are filling up fast."

"Don't let those press clippings go to your head," warned Bert. He couldn't understand why Barry got so excited at all the attention and seemed to relish the publicity he received. Bert wasn't built that way. He took it all in stride, seldom looking at the sports pages. He stayed in top condition and played hockey to the very best of his ability.

The Leafs' first long road trip took them to Montreal, Boston and New York. The twins were thrilled to find themselves on the ice at the Montreal Forum, the first NHL arena designed expressly for hockey.

"Montreal has such a rich hockey tradition," Barry said to Bert after they checked into the Windsor Hotel. Barry was reading the sports page of the *Montreal Gazette*. "There's a story in here about the city's hockey history. Did you know the first organized game was played here way back in 1875?"

"No, I didn't know that," Bert said.

"And there was a playoff game here that lasted until 2:30 in the morning," Barry continued. "The Habs and the Red Wings played six overtime periods before Detroit won by 1–0. What a marathon!"

"I pity the goalies in that game," Bert said.

"And here's another story from 1919. The Habs and the Seattle Metropolitans played for the Stanley Cup in Seattle, and most of the players became so sick they had to cancel the series."

"Sick?"

"Yeah, the flu epidemic swept across the country that spring and some of the Habs were hospitalized. One of them died. It's the only time a final series wasn't finished."

That night, the twins faced the greatest player they'd ever seen on skates—Howie Morenz. Morenz scored three goals against the Leafs, and the Habs won by a 4–3 score.

"Now I know why they call him the Babe Ruth of hockey," Bert said after the game.

Two nights later in Boston, they tangled with the Bruins' legendary defenceman, Eddie Shore.

Coach Irvin told them to keep their heads up when Shore came calling. "He's the meanest, toughest player in hockey," he warned them, "and he loves to put rookies in their place."

"Shore doesn't scare me," said Barry. "He puts his skates on one at a time—just like I do."

Late in the game, with the Leafs holding a 4–2 lead over the Bruins, Barry embarked on a solo rush and deliberately skated toward Shore. "Come on, old man, let's see what you've got," he muttered to himself.

The next thing he saw was a bank of arena lights swirling crazily overhead. His eyes blinked and watered from the string of smelling salts that was being held to his nostrils. His head cleared slowly as his vision returned. Bert was there, down on one knee, leaning in, looking concerned.

"What happened, Bert? What hit me?"

Bert rolled his eyes. "Remember what Coach Irvin told you about Eddie Shore? How he loves to put rookies in their place?"

"Yeah."

Bert tapped the ice. "Well, this is the place he put you."

By Sunday afternoon, Barry's headache was gone and he pronounced himself fit to play against the New York Rangers at Madison Square Garden. Before the game, the Kids strolled through Times Square.

"Look at the skyscrapers!" Barry said, gawking. "And the theatres, and all the bright lights. And the cabs racing around in all directions. If I ever get traded, Bert, this would be a great place for me."

Bert gave his twin a frosty look. "Sure it would. If you played here, you'd never get to bed. You'd last about six months."

At the arena, they ran into Rangers' manager Lester Patrick in the corridor.

Patrick was a hockey pioneer. He'd organized the Pacific Coast Hockey League in the twenties and built two artificial ice rinks in Vancouver and Victoria—the first in Canada. The Kids knew they were in the presence of hockey royalty and sought Patrick's autograph.

Barry had a question. "Is it true that you played goal in a Stanley Cup game a few years ago, Mr. Patrick? When you were 44 years old and retired?"

"That's true," the silver-haired gentleman said with a laugh. "I was coaching the Rangers in '28 when our goalie was injured in a playoff game against Montreal. We had no backup goalie, so I donned the pads myself. The fans howled with laughter when I skated out. And I admit I felt pretty awkward wearing those goal pads. But we won the game in overtime and we went on to win the Stanley Cup that season."

"That's pretty amazing," Bert said, impressed.

"I'm glad to meet you boys," Patrick told them. "I've heard good things about you. I wish my scouts had found you before Squint Walker signed you."

He shook hands with the Kids. "Have a good game, fellows," he said with a wink. "But not too good."

He smiled and turned away, stopping by the Rangers' dressing-room door. Then he called out to Barry. "By the way, my old friend Eddie Shore called me today. He said to give you a message."

Barry was surprised. "Oh?"

"Yes, he said you should learn to keep your head up!"

When the door closed behind him, Bert nudged his brother and burst out laughing.

Once the novelty of big-league hockey wore off, Barry became very sure of himself. He learned to keep his head up, but he also began to act like some of the NHL stars he associated with. He posed for photos and signed autographs. He joined wealthy season-ticket holders for dinner and drinks after games. A car dealer loaned him a new car to drive in return for the right to use his name in the dealer's newspaper ads.

Bert noticed the change in his twin brother, and he wasn't happy about it.

They had rented a small apartment in Toronto. At the start of the season, they were always together, just as they had been growing up. They were very close and agreed on almost everything, as most twins do. But now Barry was making friends who were fans, rather than players. He enjoyed having complete strangers clamouring to make his acquaintance.

It was in a fancy restaurant near Maple Leaf Gardens that the twins met up with Nick Ferone one night.

Ferone, well-dressed, handsome and obviously wealthy, was sitting at a nearby table with two beautiful young women. He moved across the room and introduced himself to the Kids. He told them how much he enjoyed watching them play.

"Come and join us," he said, flashing a toothy smile. "The girls are dying to meet you two."

Bert was about to decline, but he saw that Barry was eager to accept. *Why not?* he thought to himself.

Ferone and his friends were pleasant. Or at least Barry thought so. They showered the twins with compliments, and Ferone insisted on picking up the tab. Barry enjoyed their company and wondered why his brother seemed bored. By the end of the evening, Ferone and Barry had made arrangements to meet again after the next home game. Bert had caught himself stifling a yawn once or twice, and begged off the plans to meet.

From then on, Nick Ferone was part of their lives. He phoned the apartment almost every day, constantly asking for Barry. The invitations piled up, with Barry always eager to accept.

"Come with me, Bert," Barry urged, knotting his tie. "We're going to a club we've never been to before."

"Count me out, brother," Bert replied. "There's too much smoke in those clubs. And too much drinking. I want my eyes and lungs sharp for the next hockey game. You should think about that."

"Of course I think about it. But a couple of cigarettes and a cocktail or two? They're not going to kill me. And I never have to buy them. Nick pays for everything."

"Sure, and someday when Nick wants a favour—some tickets for a game, or a Leaf jersey to strut around in—you'll be the one he comes to."

"No, I won't. Nick's a friend. He wouldn't do that," Barry protested.

Bert found he was spending a lot of evenings by himself. He listened to the radio at lot and read a number of books, some of them in preparation for the courses he was planning to take in the summer. But he still missed Barry's company.

One night, Bert fell asleep on the sofa while listening to music on the radio. He woke up when he heard Barry stumble in. He could smell beer on his brother's breath.

Bert was angry. "Listen, Barry, you can't keep this up. You go out almost every night and you're coming in later and later. You're not getting enough sleep. The next thing you know, the late nights are going to affect your play on the ice."

Barry just giggled. "Lighten up, brother. You should come with me. We went dancing tonight. You'd have been proud of me, dancing around like Fred Astaire. Why, I never even went to the high school prom..."

"Sure, sure, you're a swell dancer, I'll bet. After a few beers you probably fell down and Nick had to send you home in a cab."

"How'd you know that?"

"Never mind, just get to bed. I wish you'd spend more time with the guys on the team than with playboys like Nick Ferone."

Barry belched. "Aw, the guys on the team are old... old... mud-in-the-sticks. I mean stick-in-

95

the-muds. All they talk about is hockey. They don't dance or know how to have a good time."

He burped again. "And look at you, Bert. You don't smoke or drink and you never go out. You've got to have fun when you're young. You're an old stick-in-the-mud, too."

Bert knew it was senseless to argue. "Come on. Let's get you to bed," he sighed, taking Barry by the arm. "We're on the ice at ten."

It worried Bert that Barry was spending most of his free time with Nick Ferone. Ferone seemed to have friends everywhere. The phone began ringing the moment they checked into their hotel rooms on road trips. Barry got a kick out of it, while Bert found it downright annoying, especially while he was taking his pre-game nap. Barry began skipping the naps to go out and meet the people who called.

Squint Walker and Coach Irvin began to notice a change in Barry's appearance, and his lack-adaisical play on the ice.

"What's going on?" Walker thundered one day after practice. "I hear you're ignoring the team rules. We want you rested when you get to the rink. Do I have to hire a detective to follow you around? And lately you don't have any stamina on the ice. You'd better shape up, boy."

Barry's answer to the lecture was to go out and

score the winning goal that night against the Bruins.

"Does that look like I've lost stamina?" he quipped to Bert on the way home. "I had enough stamina to go end to end and make the goalie look like a sieve."

"Yeah, well maybe if you'd had a pre-game rest you'd have scored three goals tonight," Bert countered.

Barry laughed. "And if I scored three, they'd expect three goals from me every night. No thanks! I don't need the pressure. And I don't need my coach and my manager cracking down on me. Nick says all they're interested in is keeping their own jobs."

"So Nick's an authority on hockey, is he?" Bert asked. "What else does Nick say?"

"He says that you and I form the best defence in the league, but that I've got more colour than you and that's why the crowd goes for me. He says we're both about equal in terms of playing, but I'll win rookie of the year because you're not always in the public eye like I am."

Once they were in their apartment, Bert turned to his brother. "Listen, I think Nick Ferone is a bad influence on you. How long do you think you'll last in hockey if you don't abide by the rules and show some common sense?"

"You lay off Nick," warned Barry. "He's my buddy. He knows everybody! I even heard him on the phone tonight with Harry Conklin, the Detroit manager. And he drives a great new car."

"Some buddy!" snorted Bert. "Handing you free booze and cigarettes and keeping you out at night. Squint Walker is concerned about you. He told me he's seen dozens of top young players get addicted to the bright lights and nightlife of the big city. And it destroyed some of their careers."

"So you've been yapping to Squint about me?" Barry said, with anger in his voice.

"He asked me to look out for you. I've covered up for you, thinking you'd get wise. I haven't told him how much you're drinking or how late you're getting home. But he's found out anyway, and I can't cover for you anymore."

"You're just mad because of what Nick said— about me winning the rookie award."

Bert laughed. "I don't care about the rookie award! I just don't like what's going on. I don't like your lifestyle and what it's doing to your career."

Barry leaped up. He wrenched open a dresser drawer and began cramming shirts and socks and underwear into a suitcase he hauled from the closet. "You don't like my lifestyle!" he shouted. "Then I'll take it where somebody does like it."

Bert took two strides across the room and

grabbed his brother by the arm. "Don't do this!" he said sharply. "Barry!"

Barry shook his arm away. "Shut up!" he yelled.

Barry ran into the bathroom and gathered up his shaving utensils, then threw on his overcoat.

"Listen, Barry!" Bert said. "You're making a big mistake. We've argued before and we've always worked things out. Let's sit down and talk things over."

"There's nothing to talk about. You're treating me like I don't know the ropes, like I'm in kindergarten."

"Sometimes you act like a little kid—a spoiled little kid."

"All the more reason to get out of here!"

Bert stepped in front of Barry, blocking his path to the door. "You're not going anywhere, brother."

"No? Try and stop me!" Barry lunged at Bert and shouldered him aside. Bert struck his knee on the dresser and pain shot down his leg. He limped across the room and tackled his brother just as he got to the door.

"Barry, you can't do this!"

"Oh, yes I can!" He wheeled around and struck his brother in the face with the back of his hand.

Bert went white. He didn't return the blow. A strange expression swept over his face and he stepped aside.

Barry opened the door, his suitcase in one hand, and stumbled out. Bert stared at the empty doorway. He rubbed his cheek with one hand. He could scarcely believe that his brother was gone.

CHAPTER 10

SLICK PLAYS AGAIN

Barry Mitchell did not show up at the morning skate. The trainer approached Coach Irvin and said, "Barry left a message. He said he wasn't feeling well."

The coach grunted. "Probably out late last night. He'd better show up for the game tonight. He's getting a little too big for his britches." He was angry. The Leafs were playing the Red Wings that night, and he didn't want to give his old rival, Harry Conklin, any breaks. One of his young defencemen was undisciplined, and it was bad for team morale. He'd heard from the trainer that some of the other Leafs were complaining that Barry seemed able to do pretty much as he pleased.

"Do you think that brother of yours might honour us with his presence at the game tonight?" he asked Bert acidly after the morning skate. "We'll only need him for an hour or two. Perhaps he's forgotten that we're paying him to play."

"I expect he'll be here," Bert grunted. He didn't want to mention Barry's abrupt departure from the apartment or the quarrel they'd had. "He hasn't been himself lately."

"Yes, I've noticed that. Still, it would be nice if he could spare us some time from his busy social activities. And by the way, you can tell him he's been fined 50 bucks for skipping practice. And if he fails to show tonight he'd better have a doctor's certificate stating he's near death."

"If I see him, I'll tell him," Bert replied.

Barry showed up, grim faced and surly, an hour before game time. He had nothing to say to Bert, nothing to say to anybody. Before the game was ten minutes old, Bert realized his brother was carrying his grudge right into the game itself.

Slick McCoy was at centre for the Red Wings, making his debut for the visitors. Bonesetter Bailey had finally given him permission to play.

In the warm-up, Bert could see that Slick had his shot back. Bert shouted across the ice to Barry, "Did you see that? Old Slick's back in form. I'm happy for him."

Barry pretended he didn't hear a word.

In the opening minute, Slick broke loose and rushed the puck into the Leafs' zone. Barry lunged at him and missed. Bert moved over quickly and bumped Slick off balance, but he still got a hard shot away. Broda had to be quick to snag it in his glove. He tossed it behind the net.

Barry skated in, picked up the rubber and circled his net. He looked up and saw that his wings were covered. Bert skated over, anticipating a pass.

The pass never came. Ordinarily, Barry would have flipped the puck to Bert without hesitating, paving the way for a rush out of the zone. Instead, Barry chose to battle McCoy for the puck, and suddenly the puck was on McCoy's stick, not Barry's.

"Uh oh," muttered Bert.

McCoy cut in from a sharp angle, then circled the net and came right out in front. He raised his stick—then Bert swooped in and knocked it aside before the Red Wing had a chance to shoot on Broda, who had lost his balance and was helpless. Bert raced up ice with the puck, outsmarted a Red Wing who tried to bodycheck him off stride and drilled a long pass to Blair, who carried it into the Red Wing zone.

I can't believe Barry didn't pass me the puck, Bert thought, shaking his head. *That dumb move might have cost us a goal.*

The game was hectic. The Red Wings launched a series of lightning attacks, with McCoy the spearhead of every thrust. Slick set a frantic pace, hoping to score an early goal.

In he came again, leaving Blair floundering at centre ice, whipping a pass across to his left wing. He snapped up a return pass, and like a greyhound on skates, raced into the Leaf zone. He shifted and tried to weave around Bert, couldn't find an opening and spun around, looking for another route to the net. He spotted it when Barry was slow to close the gap. Slick zipped through the hole and slammed a terrific shot past Broda to the upper corner of the net.

Slick's drive showed no apparent weakness remaining in his arm. The puck crashed into the twine and dropped to the ice as the red light flashed.

The Leafs fought back and came within an ace of scoring many times. But Mowers in the Detroit net stymied them time and again. Then came a penalty to the Leafs, and the Red Wings cut loose once more.

They concentrated on Barry's side of the ice, forcing him to work extra hard. He tried to bump them, but his timing was off. He tried to skate them into the corners, but they eluded him. He threw a bodycheck at Slick and ran headlong into the boards, while Slick slipped away, chuckling at Barry's ineptitude.

Bert attempted to cover more ice than he normally did. He worked desperately to clear the puck, to block shots, to help his goalie, to fight back the attack.

He watched helplessly as Barry began to flounder. When Barry finally stole the puck from an opposing player, he promptly coughed it up, handing it right to Abel, a Red Wing star, when Broda was sprawled in his crease with the net gaping open above him. Abel smiled as he drilled the puck over Broda. Again the red light flashed, and the visitors enjoyed a two-goal cushion.

Coach Irvin had seen enough. He yanked the Kapuskasing Kids.

In front of his teammates on the bench, Barry's coach gave him a tongue-lashing. He'd never been ripped like that in his life. But instead of appealing to his pride and making him determined to do better, it had just the opposite effect. It made him depressed and bitter. He felt sorry for himself, so he sulked.

In the second period, Barry was caught flat-footed by Danny Demers, a Detroit left winger. Demers sifted around him like he was a lawn ornament and beat Broda with a low shot to the corner. The Red Wings led by three.

Blair got the Leafs on the score sheet a few minutes later, but then McCoy came out and led another attack. Bert worked like a slave on his side of the blue line, but the Red Wings began to leave him alone, concentrating on Barry's side of the rink. Huffing and puffing, Barry lost his composure. He swung a shoulder check at McCoy so hard that he missed his man completely and fell down in a heap.

Bert raced over, but McCoy was too quick. He scooted in on goal and blasted a shot high to the corner of Broda's net.

Broda slammed his goal stick against the post. He was fuming. "That blankety-blank kid couldn't stop a peewee player!" he ranted. Bert heard him and knew exactly which player he was talking about.

The game finally ended with the Red Wings collecting six goals to the Leafs' one.

The fans left quickly, grousing about the outcome and the shortcomings the Leafs had shown—especially on defence.

Barry's performance could only be described as pitiful. And with half the famous Kid combination out to lunch, Bert's game had suffered too.

"I guess you guys aren't ready for the big time, after all," a Detroit fan taunted them as they headed for their dressing room. "You've got more holes in you than a hobo's socks."

Coach Irvin and Squint Walker could merely shake their heads after the debacle. It was the worst licking the Leafs had been handed all season.

"Did you see Harry Conklin at the end of the game?" Squint asked Irvin. "He was laughing at us. He even waved at me from across the ice—with one finger. And Slick McCoy thumbed his nose at us after he was named first star of the game."

CHAPTER 11

TROUBLE FOR BARRY

Squint Walker called Bert in for a chat after practice the next morning. "We could be in big trouble," the manager began.

"You mean with Barry," Bert said. Squint nodded.

"I've tried to talk to him, but I'm not getting through. We had a fight and now he's taken off. I don't even know where he's staying."

"What do you know about this new pal of his— Nick Ferone?" Squint asked.

"Not much. He latched onto Barry early in the season. He gives him a big buildup and plays to his ego. And he pays for everything. I'm suspicious of the guy."

"You should be. I've done some checking, and this Ferone guy has served some jail time. He's been associated with well-known gamblers. One of them is notorious—Fats Fogel. Remember five or six years ago... or you might have been too young. Anyway, two kids were kicked out of hockey for life for getting involved in gambling. They laid bets with Fats Fogel on the outcome of games they played in."

"I didn't know that. That's serious stuff. But Barry would never do that. He's never gambled in his life. And I'm sure he doesn't know Fats Fogel."

"Hmm, I hope you're right." The manager paused to sip his coffee. "Listen, Bert. I want my Leafs to be squeaky clean. No scandals. And I'm worried that your brother is headed for trouble."

"I sure hope not," said Bert. "I'll talk to him again."

"No, I'll talk to him. And when I do, he's not going to like it. I'm going to send him to the minors for a while. Maybe he'll get the message."

Bert was not surprised. "I'd hate to see him go, although I suppose it could be the best thing for him. But why not give him one more chance? Don't send him to Rochester right now. Bring him along on the road trip to Chicago and see if he's changed. I'll try to knock some sense into him."

Walker tapped his fingers on the desk while he made a decision. "I'll do it for you, Bert. But it's his last chance. If Barry doesn't play well in Chicago, he's gone."

Later that day, Squirt called Barry on the carpet. The manager was calm but very serious. "I'm disappointed in you, Barry," he began. "You're not pulling your weight on my team. And I don't like to see you hanging around with Nick Ferone. He's a gambler and a con man, and I think he may be conning you."

"Wait a minute!" Barry protested. "You're knocking my best friend. I can tell you he's not a gambler—I'm not dumb enough to hang around with gamblers!"

Squint was annoyed at Barry's tone of voice. "Maybe he isn't, I don't know," he said gruffly. "But I hear he associates with gamblers, and where there's smoke there's often fire. He runs with guys who wager on sporting events, and that's all it takes to tar a guy with the same brush. I'm warning you—stay away from Ferone.

"And here's another thing," Walker continued, holding his fingers close together. "Your play has fallen off, and you're about this far from going down to Rochester. If you don't like the NHL, we'll see how you enjoy playing in the American League. There'll be less money and long bus rides."

Barry sat up. "You'd send me to the minors?" he croaked. The idea had never occurred to him.

"Why not? You're only half the player you were early in the season. It takes hard work to make it to the NHL, and it takes hard work to stay here. You haven't been working, you've been partying and gallivanting all over town. And you're playing with fire when you hang around with fellows like Ferone. You'd be on your way to Rochester at this moment if your brother hadn't talked me into giving you another chance. But it's your last chance. If you turn in another lousy game in Chicago, you're gone. Now get out of here—I've got to start looking for someone to replace you."

Barry was in shock when he left the office. He didn't really believe Walker would send him to Rochester. He must have been kidding. It must be a bluff. Hadn't all the sportswriters raved about him since the season opened? Hadn't they said he was one of the best young prospects in the game? Still, he was a little concerned about what Walker had told him about Nick Ferone.

Ferone played poker once in a while—he knew that. But they were just friendly games for nickels and dimes. That could hardly be called gambling. Sure, Nick had many friends, and there could be a few gamblers among them. And he went to the track and bet on the ponies. But there was nothing wrong with that, nothing illegal. He knew that betting on hockey games could present a problem. If a player was caught doing it, he could end up with a lifetime suspension. *But I'd never do that,* Barry thought.

He decided to come right out and ask his friend

Nick about the accusations. But when he tried to reach him, no one answered the phone. He still hadn't been able to contact him when the Leafs left on the train for the Windy City.

On the train, Barry opted not to sit with Bert. He sat by himself, reading a book. Bert could only shrug. He sat next to Coach Irvin for part of the journey and listened to his stories.

"When I was a player in the Western League," the coach told him. "I scored 31 goals in 30 games. You won't believe the name of my team. It was the Portland Rosebuds. Imagine naming a team the Rosebuds! That year, the owner of the Chicago Black Hawks bought the Portland club and moved all of the players into Chicago. I was named team captain, but the owner, Major McLaughlin, had no patience with his coaches. He hired ten of them in the next few years.

"One of them, a fellow named Matheson, he met on a train. Major McLaughlin was impressed when Matheson told him he'd led a midget team in Winnipeg to a championship."

"A midget team?" marvelled Bert. "And he became a coach in the NHL?"

Irvin chuckled. "He did. And in his first practice session, he stepped on the ice wearing shin pads outside his pants, elbow pads on his knees and a cap with tassels on his head. The players could barely control their laughter. And then he ordered them not to shoot pucks at our goalie for fear they'd injure him with their shots.

"Then he came up with another bright idea. He told his smallest forward, Mush March, to lead a rush and try to split the defence. At the last second, he ordered March to drop the puck back to Taffy Abel, a huge defenceman. March would open the hole, and Abel would dash through it and score."

"And did it work?" asked Bert, captivated by the story.

"Of course not. Poor March was about the size of a button. He hit the defence and got squashed. And Abel couldn't score even if he did get through. He averaged only two goals a season in five years."

Bert was amused. "That's some coaching!" he said. "Did Matheson last the season?"

"He only lasted two games," Irvin replied. "He came up with another bright idea and it cost him his job. He invented a system of whistle-blowing to use from the bench. He'd signal plays by blowing a whistle. One blast meant the puck carrier should pass the puck, two blasts called for him to shoot on goal, three toots on the whistle meant to turn and backcheck... and so on. It was the most bizarre, bewildering strategy ever conceived."

"Did he do that in a game?" Bert asked. "I imagine

it would drive the referee crazy, not to mention the fans."

"He never got a chance," Irvin said. "He was about to coach his third game when Major McLaughlin ran up to him and said, 'Matheson, you're fired. Pack your bags and get out of town, and take that darn whistle with you.'"

If anyone but the coach had told him these hockey stories, Bert wouldn't have believed him. But Coach Irvin had been there, had played in Chicago.

The coach went on to tell Bert some other stories about the Chicago franchise, and ended with one about the Hawks' all-star goaltender, Charlie Gardiner.

"Charlie was a great little goalie, but he had no backup. When we practiced, the net at the other end of the rink was always empty. One day, Major McLaughlin told us he'd invented a backup goalie. He'd ordered someone to stuff a large bag full of straw and shape it into a figure like a scarecrow. He even put a belt around the dummy's middle. Then he had the scarecrow—the dummy goalie— strung up in the net. Players blistered him with shots, trying to knock the stuffing out of him, but they couldn't do it. They began teasing Charlie: 'Hey, Charlie, that dummy's looking better every day. He never yaps at us for not clearing the puck.

And you can't fake him to the ice like some goalies we know.' Things like that."

Bert laughed out loud, imaging the scene.

"When one of the Hawks said, 'That dummy's smarter than Charlie. Better looking, too. I hear the Major is going to send Gardiner down and replace him with the straw man,' Charlie had had enough."

"What did he do?"

"He ripped the dummy from the net, hauled him into the dressing room and told the trainer, 'Give this guy a rubdown. He's falling to pieces out there. Then give him a few bucks for a beer and a sandwich and get him out of town! The guy is really beginning to bug me.'"

Bert was still smiling when he climbed into his upper berth an hour later.

Meanwhile, Barry was determined to make a good showing against the Black Hawks. Bluff or no bluff, he didn't want to be shipped to the minors.

Earlier in the season, he had always shared a room on the road with Bert. Since their fight, Barry had requested a change, and his new roommate was Murrow, a quiet forward who read nothing but comic books and made long-distance phone calls to a girl named Myrtle somewhere back in Manitoba.

Barry didn't see Bert until he showed up in the

dressing room in the dingy bowels of the vast Chicago Stadium. In spite of what Walker had told him, he reckoned that Bert was behind the threat to send him to the minors. It must have been Bert who talked to the manager about Nick Ferone and what a shady character he was.

When they had both finished dressing, Bert slid along the bench until he was next to Barry. "How are you doing, kid?" he asked.

"I'm okay."

"Good. Let's stick together like we used to and knock the Black Hawks cockeyed tonight."

"Look," said Barry, "why don't you look after your side of the ice and I'll look after mine? I don't want to get too close to a squealer."

Bert was shocked into silence. Did his brother really think of him as a squealer? He shook his head. He started to say something, then thought better of it.

"Sure, kid," he said. He got up and walked away.

Barry didn't look after his side of the ice very well that night. He played a lacklustre game. The impressive way he had teamed up with his brother had vanished. The skills that once caught the eye of every fan were gone. The cohesion that made the Kapuskasing Kids the talk of the league was invisible.

The Black Hawks saw an opportunity and pounced on it. They pumped in two goals in the first period, while the Kids were on the ice, and added two more in the second. Barry showed all the charisma of a fire hydrant in his attempts to stop the second-period goals.

In the third period, Hawk centre Max Bentley won a faceoff and passed to Mosienko, who sped around his check and swooped in over the blue line. Barry was in his path and tried to ride him to the boards. But Mosienko had real speed and couldn't be stopped. He wiggled away from Barry's lunge and drove a whistling shot at Broda. The puck hit the goalie in the chest and bounded away. Mosienko chased after it and snapped a pass over to Doug Bentley, who was waiting in the slot, ready to pounce. Barry tried to intercept, swung and missed. First he lost his balance and almost went down. Then he lost his head. Realizing he'd been outfoxed, he savagely stepped into Mosienko, seconds after the Chicago player had passed the puck. He lifted his knee into Mosienko's groin and caught him across the jaw with his upraised stick. Mosienko fell to the ice as if he'd tumbled off a diving board. He lay in a heap on the ice while 15,000 voices shouted their disapproval.

"Boo! Boo! Booooo!" Debris from the stands

hurtled toward Barry—hats, coins and a flurry of programs. A pair of toe rubbers landed in Broda's goal crease, and he picked them up to check if they were his size.

Mosienko didn't move. Players from both teams gathered around him. The swift little winger was one of the league's cleanest, most popular players.

The referee glared at Barry and thumbed him to the penalty box. "Major penalty, five minutes," he ruled. Then he looked Barry straight in the eye and said, "Dirty play, kid. I didn't expect that from you."

Barry did not return to the ice. When his penalty expired, Coach Irvin sent him to the dressing room. "Get showered and get dressed," he barked. "You're finished around here."

Mosienko came back in time to throw in another goal. He set up two more for the Bentleys, and the game ended with Chicago winning by a 7–1 score.

Barry was already in his street clothes, chewing on an orange, when Squint Walker strode into the dressing room. "You're gone," he declared. "Don't say I didn't warn you."

"Gone? Gone where?"

"As if you don't know," sneered the manager. "When we get back to Toronto, there'll be a ticket waiting for you. Your next stop is Rochester. Report there on Tuesday."

Barry threw the orange at the wall. "Hey, what if I don't feel like reporting to Rochester?"

Walker spun around and glared at the rookie. "That'll be just too bad, won't it? Because then you won't be playing for anybody. I'll see that you're blackballed from every team in the universe."

"Wait a minute!" argued Barry. "Why not trade me? Lots of clubs would love to have me."

Walker snorted. "That's what you think. I've asked around and nobody wants you. You've got a reputation as a playboy and a first-class rebel. No big-league team wants a player who won't abide by club rules. That lets you out. Go to the minors or go home."

Walker stormed out of the room, slamming the dressing room door behind him.

Barry sucked on another orange and stared at the floor. Silently, his teammates undressed and headed for the shower stalls. Bert got up and walked over.

"Barry," he said, almost in a whisper, "I'm really sorry this happened. But lots of young players spend time in the minors. You'll be back before you know it. A couple of weeks in Rochester..."

Barry lifted his head, and stared straight into his brother's blue eyes. "Let's get one thing straight, Bert. I am not reporting to Rochester." He turned, grabbed his overcoat and headed for the door. "And I won't be seeing you again. Not unless I'm playing against you."

He walked out into the night.

Bert sat down. He shook his head, wondering how things that had looked so promising only a few months earlier had suddenly gone so wrong.

Buddy Broda came over and put a hand on Bert's shoulder. "I know it's rough on you," said the goalie, "but he's just upset. He'll report to Rochester, all right. Once he thinks it over, he'll cool down."

"I hope so," muttered Bert. "I have no idea how I'm going to explain this to my folks."

CHAPTER 12

BARRY DISAPPEARS

On the long overnight train ride back to Toronto, Barry kept to himself. He refused to meet the eyes of any of his teammates, and especially not his brother. He climbed straight into his upper berth, switched on the overhead light and began to read, but he couldn't concentrate on the words. A tear dropped from one eye. It surprised him, and he wiped it away. Then he began to realize just how miserable he felt.

He wondered what he should do. Initially, he'd vowed to tear up the ticket to Rochester and defy his bosses, but common sense eventually took over. There was no sense burning his bridges completely. He would have to report in two days, despite his threat not to. If he didn't, he'd face a suspension by the league. It was all spelled out in his contract.

During the train ride, he did some hard thinking about Nick Ferone. He had some questions to ask him. He wanted to meet with Ferone, but he didn't have much time.

He sighed and began to regret his flare-up with Squint Walker. He realized that his ego had been badly damaged, but he knew he couldn't blame Squint, who'd been a friend and mentor and had given the kids a chance to play in the NHL with a great team. Barry began to understand why Squint was upset. The Kids had let him down. No, *he* had let him down—not Bert. Bert was blameless. Bert never let anyone down.

He sighed again and went back to his book. *I've loused up everything*, he told himself finally.

He tossed and turned most of the night, and when the train arrived at Toronto's cavernous Union Station in the early hours of the morning, he realized he had slept right through the porter's wake-up call. He scrambled into his clothes and found that the other players had already left the train and the station.

Why didn't Bert wake me like he usually does? Barry thought to himself. And when he realized why, he felt foolish. Barry had wanted to make peace with Bert, but Bert was gone.

He decided to go straight to Nick Ferone's apartment, where he'd been staying in a spare bedroom, then visit Bert before leaving for Rochester—if he'd even speak to him.

He phoned Ferone, who greeted him cheerfully. "Hi pal, are you back from Chicago?"

"I just got in, Nick. I'm going to come by and pick up my stuff. They're sending me to the minors."

"Gee, I'm sorry to hear that," Ferone replied. "Squint Walker must have rocks in his head."

"It won't be for long, Nick. I guarantee you that."

"That's the spirit. Say, let me come down and pick you up. We'll have breakfast at a place I know. I want you to meet a friend of mine."

Barry hesitated. Then he said, "All right. I'll meet you in front of the station."

Twenty minutes later, Nick pulled up in a big black sedan, and Barry hopped into the passenger's seat.

Nick drove west to the outskirts of the city.

"Where are we going?" Barry asked.

"My pal breeds horses. He has a horse farm out here." Nick winked at Barry. "He's rolling in money, and he loves the way you play hockey. He won't believe that Walker's sending you down."

Nick turned into a long lane and drove up to a mansion. A servant opened the front door and ushered them in, where they were greeted by a heavyset man with a florid face and oily black hair. He shook hands with Barry and patted him on the shoulder. "I've been wanting to meet you, son," he said. "I'm a big fan. Come and sit down. The chef has breakfast ready, and we can have a good chat."

Nick pulled a camera out of his pocket. "Before we eat, I'd like to get a photo of the two of you together. What do you say?"

"Sure," said Barry, who'd already posed for dozens of similar shots in his brief career. He threw one arm around the host's shoulder and smiled at the camera.

Click! Click! Click!

"Thanks," Nick said. "I got three good ones!"

Barry nudged his friend. "Nick, you forgot to introduce us."

"You're right, Barry," Nick answered. "Say hello to Fats Fogel."

Barry recognized the name, and his heart began to pound. This was the big-time gambler he'd been warned about. Two hockey players had seen their careers ended just for associating with this man. What was going on? Why had Nick brought him to this place? He felt like he'd been duped.

"Sit down, boys," Fogel suggested. "Let's have breakfast."

Barry's mind was in turmoil. He didn't want breakfast. "Could I see your horse barn first?" he asked. "I love horses. And I need to talk to Nick for a moment."

"Sure," agreed Fogel. "Show him around, Nick. Then we'll eat."

As they left the house, Barry noticed two photos on the wall. One was of a hockey player, while the other appeared to be of an executive of some kind. "Why, that's Slick McCoy!" he said aloud. "I thought you were a Leaf fan, Mr. Fogel."

"Oh, I am," he answered, "except when the Red Wings are in town. My brother-in-law is the Detroit manager, Harry Conklin."

Barry was stunned. He read the inscription on Conklin's photo: *To my pal Fats. You can always bet on Detroit, ha ha! Best wishes, Harry Conklin.*

Then Barry peered at the inscription on Slick's photo. It read: *To Fats. Thanks for your hospitality and support! Slick McCoy.*

Barry turned and hurried out of the house. He felt nauseated.

When they had reached the horse barn, Barry pulled on Nick's sleeve, throwing him off balance. "We have to talk," he said urgently. "There are some things I don't understand. Squint Walker is worried about our relationship."

Nick didn't appear to be surprised. "Is that so? What's he so worried about?"

"He says you may be mixed up with big-time gamblers," Bert explained.

Nick laughed out loud. "What a prissy little

man! Since when is gambling a crime?"

"It's not, of course. But it's not good when hockey players are involved," Barry countered. He gestured toward the mansion. "You know who that guy is, don't you?"

"Of course I do," said Nick, his eyes growing suddenly cold. "Fats Fogel is a pretty famous guy."

"Famous as a big-time gambler."

"So what?" Nick asked belligerently.

"So what! Don't you see? He could ruin my career."

"Wake up, will you, kid? Your career is already in ruins. You're on your way to the minors." Barry was shocked at Nick's tone. It was definitely no longer friendly.

Barry began to get angry. "Let's get out of here! I can't have breakfast with a shady character like Fogel. We'll talk in the car." Out of the corner of his eye, he noticed two men dressed in denim overalls enter the barn. Farmhands?

"Not so fast, busher," Nick said. His eyes had narrowed. "I'll drive you back, but first you've got to make me a little promise."

"A promise? What kind of promise?" Barry was getting edgy.

"Here's what you're going to do for me. You're going to serve your time in the minors, prove yourself and jump back to the Leafs. Then I want you to take it easy whenever you face the Red Wings."

"You what? What do you mean?"

"It means you let the Wings get past you for a goal or two. Instead of blocking shots, you let them go through your legs. If a Red Wing elbows you, you go down. And he goes in to score. You see what I mean? And if you have a breakaway, you shoot the puck wide of the net, not into it."

Barry was boiling mad. "Are you crazy? That's fixing games—I'd be thrown out for life. I'd never do that!"

Nick laughed and held up the camera. "Sure you would, if you were afraid that your photo might appear in all the papers, with you standing next to the gambling king of the sports world."

Barry's eyes widened as he remembered the photo Nick had taken in the kitchen. The papers would love to print that. He had to get his hands on the film. He lunged at Nick and grabbed him by the arm. He easily pulled the camera from his grasp and threw it to the ground, then stomped on it until it shattered.

"There!" he gasped in relief. "Now there's no evidence that I ever met Fogel."

Nick didn't seem concerned. He laughed and called the two farmhands over. "Here!" he called out. "Hang onto this." He pulled a roll of film from his pocket and tossed it high in the air. One of the farmhands caught it and put it in the pocket of his overalls.

"Son of a…" Barry threw himself at the farmhand. And that's about all he remembered. The farmhand lashed out and punched him right in the nose. Then both men threw him to the ground and began punching him and kicking him. One of them whacked Barry over the head with the handle of a broom. In minutes, he was a bloody mess, an inert form sprawled in the hay that littered the floor. Nick knelt and felt for a pulse.

"He's alive, but barely," he told them. "You didn't have to hit him that hard." Nick wiped his hands. He didn't want to be a party to a murder. The two thugs he'd hired weren't so concerned. They were so accustomed to dirty work that violence and brutality were second nature to them.

"What'll we do with him now, Nick?" one of the brutes asked, examining his bloody knuckles. "Finish him off?"

Nick thought for a moment. He hadn't expected the kid to fight back. Now, when Barry came to, he would go straight to the police. Nick couldn't allow that to happen. He never wanted to see the inside of a jail cell again.

"No, not here," Nick answered. "I'll tell you

what. There's a car parked behind the barn. Take his wallet and any identification he has on him, wrap him in a horse blanket, then throw him in the car and drive him away from here. Go north at least 100 miles to a little town called Boonville. I grew up there. You'll find lots of woods and gullies nearby. When it gets dark, finish him off and toss him in the woods—deep in the woods."

The thugs grinned. "Sounds good," said one. "It's a nice day for a drive in the country."

"Here's your film," said the other, fishing in his pocket. He tossed the roll to Nick.

Nick had one more request. "If you drive through Boonville, stop at Mother Fitcher's Bakery. She makes the best blueberry pie in the country. Pick up one for me and buy one for yourselves. You won't regret it. I'll see you later."

Nick returned to the house to find Fats Fogel finishing off a huge breakfast. Part of a scrambled egg fell from his mouth as Nick entered.

"Where's our boy?" Fats asked.

"He's gone," Nick replied with a half smile. "Gone forever if you know what I mean. He refused to do what I told him to do."

"That's too bad," said Fats, slurping coffee from a cup. "I liked that boy. He was a player, a solid defenceman." He chuckled. "Well, he was until you started corrupting him."

Nick held up the roll of film. "I'll get this developed in a few days. I'll pick out a good one of you and Barry together, and I'll get it blown up and framed for your collection. Anyway, you can tell Harry Conklin and Slick McCoy that they won't have to worry about one of the Kids anymore. And tell Harry to send the money he promised me."

CHAPTER 13

MAX AND MARTY ARRIVE

A couple of days passed, and Bert Mitchell was frantic with worry. His brother Barry seemed to have disappeared off the face of the planet. Squint Walker and Coach Irvin and most of the players figured Barry had deserted the club deliberately.

"He's hot-tempered and stubborn, but I don't think he'd do that," Bert said. "I think something bad has happened to him."

"Aw, he's just ticked off because I sent him down to Rochester," said the manager. "He'll show up one day soon after he's had time to think things over. Meanwhile, I've had to suspend him. I had no choice."

"What'll you tell the reporters?" asked Bert.

"I've already told them your brother was under a lot of stress and needed some time off for personal reasons. I said a brief stint in Rochester might do him some good, but it might be a few days before he reported there. And I asked them to show some empathy and take it easy on him."

"Do you think I should call the police and file a missing person's report?"

"Not yet, Bert. Give Barry a day or two more to show up."

His brother's mysterious disappearance began to affect Bert's play on the ice. Sick with worry, his mind wandered and his reactions were sluggish. For the first time in his brief career, he was booed in a couple of games, and he heard from the critics.

"Get the lead out, Mitchell! Go back to Kapuskasing!"

Squint Walker took him aside after two straight losses. "You're way off form," he told him. "You're worrying too much about Barry, but you've got your own life to live now. If he chooses to throw his career away, that's his funeral. You don't have to do the same."

But Bert couldn't ignore the situation. "I can't sleep, Squint. It's the suspense that's getting to me. Maybe he didn't clear out on purpose. I talked to Nick Ferone, and he says Barry never came back for his belongings. He says he hasn't seen Barry since he left on the trip to Chicago."

"Do you think Nick's lying?"

"Why would he lie?"

"Listen, if your brother were kidnapped or in a car accident, we'd have heard about it. The police would have called, right?"

"Right."

"Now, I've got more bad news for you, kid," the manager said. "The team owner called me in today and asked me what I planned to do with you. He wanted to know why you were playing such lousy hockey—his words, not mine."

Bert looked Squint in the eyes. "And...?"

"I told him that if you didn't play up to your old form against the Bruins tonight I would send you down to Rochester and bring Kramer up to replace you. I hate to do this to you, Bert, but my job's on the line if I don't."

Bert sighed. "I understand. Maybe I'm just not cut out to be a big-league hockey player."

"Oh, you're cut out for it, all right. You're just in a slump. And we all know why."

Before he left his apartment for the game that night, Bert received a phone call from home.

Big Ed's voice sounded surprisingly strong. "You asked me to call if Barry showed up back here. Well, he hasn't, and I'd like to know what's going on down there. I brought you boys up to be good, smart hockey players, and decent individuals off the ice. Just as soon as you get off to a good start, Barry gets himself suspended. And now you tell

133

me he's run off somewhere and nobody's heard from him."

"That's right, Dad…"

"You promised your mother you'd look after Barry, and it looks like you fell down on the job. And I see that you haven't been playing so well lately. I should have known better than to let you two go off chasing your hockey dreams. Young fellows like you get all caught up in the glamour of the NHL and then they forget everything they've ever been taught. I want you to find Barry and straighten him out. If you don't, I'll hop on a train and come down there and do it myself."

"I'll do my best, Dad," Bert promised. "Now put Mom on for a minute."

Bert was almost in tears when he heard his mother's voice. "Mom, I'm real sorry that I didn't take better care of Barry. He just vanished. And don't tell Dad, because it'll really upset him, but if I don't play well tonight I may be headed for the minors, too."

"Oh, son, what a shame. But I'm sure you'll do well tonight."

"And if they send me to Rochester, who's going to look for Barry? Dad's not well enough yet—I don't want him coming down here."

His mother sighed. "Listen, I have an idea," she told him. "I think I know who might be able to take a trip to the city for a few days and play detective."

By the time Bert suited up for the game that night against the Bruins, his mental strain had increased 100 percent. If he'd been a little older, a little more experienced, he might have been able to put aside his personal problems, might have been able to focus only on the game and his performance in it.

He tried hard to focus, because he knew that his hopes of staying with the Leafs depended on a first-class effort. But as luck would have it, the Bruins were on a roll, coasting along on a five-game winning streak. The Leafs, on the other hand, were struggling to emerge from a horrible slump. They'd won only two of their last eight games.

The Bruins' big line of Cowley, Smith and Conacher dominated the first period and toyed with the Leafs' checking line.

Cowley raced in, and Bert, looking grim and high-strung, tried to bump him off the puck. But his timing was bad and Cowley sifted through to score a pretty goal. "You're not so hot without your brother," one of the Bruins taunted Bert as he skated back to centre ice. "In fact, you're not so hot, period."

The Bruins scored two more goals in the second period, both while Bert was on the ice. And in the third, from a faceoff to the left of the Leaf goal, Cowley won the draw and let fly a high, hard shot. Bert got the blade of his stick on the puck and was stunned to see it change direction and sail into the upper corner of the net.

Buddy Broda didn't have a chance. The goalie smashed his stick against the goal post and glared at Bert. "Let me handle those high shots," he said hotly. "I would have had that one. The last thing I need is my own players scoring on me!"

"Geez, I'm sorry, Buddy," Bert muttered, feeling sick to his stomach.

The deflection wrecked whatever confidence Bert had left, and the fans showered him with abuse. The Leafs didn't score a goal and were handed another drubbing, 7–0 on home ice.

After the game, Mr. Smythe, the team owner, found Squint Walker. "I'm paying you to make the hard decisions," he barked. "What are you going to do?"

"I'll make changes," Squint answered.

"You'd better. We can't expect to win all the games, but we can't keep losing like this. It's unacceptable. And when we do, I sometimes get the idea that my manager doesn't know the hockey business."

The next morning, Bert got a phone call. He was told to report to Rochester.

Bert was packing when he heard a knock on his door. When he opened it, there stood Max and Marty Mitchell, his cousins from Indian River. He was amazed to see them. "Hey, guys, what are you doing here?"

"We came down on the overnight train," Max explained. "Your mom called last night and told us about Barry. She thought we could help in the search. We called to tell you we were coming, but of course you were at the hockey game, so there was no answer."

"Come on in." Bert said. "It's good to see you, but I've just had bad news." He nodded at his half-packed suitcase. "I've got to report to Rochester right away. If you plan to stay a few days, you can bunk in here."

While he finished packing, Bert filled them in on the events leading up to Barry's disappearance. Then he looked at his watch. "I've got to run," he said. "I'm late."

He shook their hands and said goodbye. "My keys are on my dresser," he shouted when he was out the door and halfway down the stairs. "And my car is parked out back—it's an old blue Chev coupe. You've got a driver's licence, don't you, Max?"

Max assured him he did, as Bert gave them a salute, ran down the stairs and was gone.

"We'll have to work fast," Marty said. "Dad told us we could only have a couple of days away from school. So where will we start? There aren't any clues. It's like looking for a needle in a haystack."

"Let's think," Max answered. "Bert mentioned that fellow Nick Ferone. He was Barry's closest friend. And he sounds like a shady character. Let's start with him—maybe he's helping Barry hide. I'll bet his address is around here somewhere."

Nick lived alone in a small house with an attached garage in the city's west end. He wasn't expecting visitors, so he was surprised to hear the doorbell ring and find two teenagers standing on his front porch.

"Whatever you're selling, I don't want any," Nick said rudely. He began to shut the door in their faces.

"Wait a minute, Mr. Ferone. I'm Max Mitchell, and this is my brother, Marty," Max said politely. "We're looking for our cousin Barry Mitchell, the hockey player. We thought you might be able to help us."

"Sorry, bud," Ferone answered. "I haven't seen your cousin in days. I already told his brother."

He was about to close the door when Max said,

"Wait! Bert said Barry might have left a few of his things here. Can we come in and pick them up?"

Ferone hesitated a moment, then said, "Yeah, I guess. He left some stuff in my spare bedroom. Come on in—the room's over there. I put all his clothes in a suitcase. I figure he isn't coming back."

The boys entered the small room and spotted the suitcase on the floor. Max picked it up and had turned to leave when Marty touched him on the elbow.

"Look at all these photos on the wall," Marty said. "Nick Ferone was quite a hockey player when he was a kid. And it looks like he played for teams in Boonville. There's a Boonville crest on all of his jerseys."

"That's north of here somewhere," Max said, steering his brother from the room. Ferone was waiting for them in the kitchen.

"So you have no idea where we might look for Barry?" Max asked Ferone. "Our family is pretty upset that he's missing."

"Not a clue." Ferone declared, looking away. "The kid could be anywhere."

He's nervous, Max thought to himself. *Why is he nervous? I think he's lying.*

"Barry didn't leave a note?" Marty asked.

"No. No note." Ferone began to fidget.

139

Max spoke boldly. "Come on, Mr. Ferone. You must have some idea where he is."

"I'm telling you, I don't know. He could be anywhere between here and Boon... I mean Timbuctoo."

Max looked around and saw a large white box lying open on the kitchen counter. It made him curious. "May I have a glass of water before we go?" he asked.

"Yeah, okay. There's a clean glass on the counter."

While he drank, Max examined the white box out of the corner of his eye. On its side were the words "Mother Fitcher's Bakery, Boonville."

It's a large pie box containing a half-finished blueberry pie, Max surmised. *And it obviously came from Boonville.*

CHAPTER 14

FINDING BARRY

Barry Mitchell climbed slowly out of bed, went to the bathroom and stared at his face in the mirror over the sink. "What a mess," he muttered before going back to bed. He lay on his back and stared at the ceiling. Gingerly, he put a hand to his face. His eyes were black and puffy. His nose was broken and covered with white surgical tape. He had a headache and his stomach muscles were bruised. He hoped his ribs weren't broken.

No wonder nobody has recognized me, he thought. *I took quite a beating. I'm lucky to be alive.* So much had happened in the past day, and he couldn't remember a lot of it.

He recalled waking up and shivering. He was outdoors, in the woods, and he was extremely cold. Blood had matted to his face. He was wrapped in what looked to be a horse blanket, and the little protection it provided had probably kept him from freezing to death.

He vaguely remembered two heavyset men carrying him along a path that led deep into the woods and dropping him roughly into a shallow ditch. He heard one of the men say to the other, "Let's finish him off now, like Nick said. Have you got your gun?"

"I've got my gun."

"Then shoot him. Nobody will hear. Then we'll kick some dirt over him."

Barry shuddered. He heard a pistol being cocked.

"Aw, look at him," a voice said—the man with the pistol. "He's finished. And if he isn't, he soon will be. He'll freeze to death out here. There's no need to shoot him."

"You're right. It'll look more like an accident if he freezes stiff."

"And we wouldn't be able to kick dirt over his body. The ground's frozen solid."

The men turned and walked away. Barry must have lost consciousness after that.

It was early morning when he awoke. He crawled from the blanket and staggered to his feet. His head was spinning, his fingers were frost-bitten, every muscle in his body ached and his throat was dry. He thought surely he was about to throw up.

He heard sounds of water bubbling over rocks

and made his way to a nearby brook. After he scooped up some water in his hands and drank greedily, he felt better.

He noticed that his pockets had been turned inside out. His wallet was gone, along with his keys and his driver's licence—Nick's thugs had taken everything.

He thought about calling out for help, but he realized no one would hear. Besides, his assailants might still be lurking nearby. He found the path the men had followed to bring him to the remote place. He wasn't thinking clearly or he would have wrapped himself in the blanket, but he left it behind.

Barry followed the path through the woods, moving slowly, a few feet at a time. He stumbled over a log and fell, throwing one hand out to protect his aching ribs. He cried out in pain. The trail seemed never-ending, but then it suddenly gave way to a grassy field, covered with patches of snow. He figured it had taken him about an hour to get that far.

He climbed down the slope of a hill and wound up in a gravel ditch. He heard the rumble of an 18-wheeler whooshing by and knew he was close to a highway. After sloshing through the frigid water in the ditch, he crawled up another slope and there it was. He hesitated for a moment, trying to decide which way to go. He shrugged, turned right and stumbled along the side of the highway. He looked back over his shoulder several times, hoping to hear the sound of an oncoming truck or car. Nothing. He felt dizzy and fell to his knees several times. Just when he had decided he couldn't take another step, he felt strong arms grab him by the waist. Someone was holding him up. He blinked and looked up, confused. Beside him was a big man in overalls and a plaid jacket, wearing a John Deere cap on his head. A farmer, he guessed.

"You're coming with me, young fellow," the man told him. "My name's Fraser. We'll get you to the house and call Doc Green. It looks like somebody ran right over you with a car."

He woke up in a small bedroom with Doc Green looking over him. The doctor examined Barry's injuries, then sat down in a chair beside the bed. "I've seen worse," the doctor told him. "Your face is a mess, but time will cure that. Your ribs are bruised, but I don't think they're broken. And you won't lose any fingers. You're pretty beaten up, and exposure almost got you. And you seem to have a concussion. Were you hitchhiking? Did some reckless driver smack into you on the highway?"

"Uh, I don't remember," Barry murmured.

"Did somebody throw you from a car?"

Barry shook his head. "I don't remember. I don't think so."

Barry needed time to think. Doc Green would be calling in the police. The police would want to know who he was. And when they learned he was Barry Mitchell, NHL defenceman, the reporters would arrive in droves. For now, it was best he didn't remember much of anything.

"You get some rest," the doctor ordered. "You seem to have suffered a little memory loss. Do you know if you have family around here—in Boonville perhaps? I should notify them."

Barry shrugged and shook his head. "No. No family."

The doctor stood up. "Well, you're in good hands with the Frasers. It's lucky Ben Fraser spotted you from the window and ran out to haul you in. We don't have a hospital here in Boonville. Maybe we should send you by ambulance to Toronto..."

Barry shook his head. "No, don't do that. I'll be fine. I like it here."

"Surely you remember your name, son?" the doctor asked. "Your pockets were empty. You weren't carrying a wallet."

Barry had been looking out the window a moment earlier and seen a big red barn. "My name's Barns, sir. Robert Barns. But you can call me Red. Red's my nickname."

"Hmmm. Red Barns," mused the doctor. "An odd name. Well, you get some sleep. A constable with the provincial police may stop around tomorrow to ask you some questions."

I'm trying to get some sleep, Barry thought as he lay in bed, *but it's hard when I have no idea what I'm going to do when people figure out who I am, or whether Bert has even noticed that I'm gone.*

When the constable, an officer named Cherry, stopped by the following morning, Barry was sitting up in bed. The constable asked him some questions and made some notes.

"Doc Green says your memory's a bit fuzzy. Were you hitchhiking?"

"Maybe. I guess so."

"Perhaps somebody got out of their car, beat you up and stole your money. Maybe two or three fellows. Does that make sense?"

"Could be. It seems to me there were two fellows. But I can't really remember."

"Whoever did it could be 100 miles from here by now. Do you have family you want me to call? A boss, maybe?"

"No, my family's all gone. At least I think so. No boss."

"All right, then. I'll wait until you're feeling

better. The doctor says your memory should come back at any minute."

"Thank you, officer."

Barry had been staying with the Frasers and avoiding Doc Green's questions for a couple days when Max and Marty arrived in Boonville following their conversation with Ferone. Less than a mile away from the Fraser farm, they stood in the town post office, asking questions of residents as they came in to collect their mail.

"We're looking for a friend of ours—a cousin actually," Max asked anyone who paused to listen. He held up a photo of Barry. "He's missing. We wonder if you've seen a stranger in town, a young guy about 20—blondish hair, good looking, a strong guy."

All of them looked at the photo for a moment, then shook their heads. The boys moved on to the grocery store and asked more questions. No luck there, either. They got the same result at the hardware store and at the barbershop.

"We've reached a dead end," Max said as they drove down the main street.

"Why don't we try looking around outside town? Maybe Ferone's hiding Barry in a cabin in the woods somewhere," Marty suggested.

"Good idea, Marty," said Max.

They left Bert's car at the side of the road and began exploring the woods on foot, wrapped up in layers of winter clothing to keep them warm in the freezing temperatures. They had been following various paths for over an hour before Marty suddenly stopped.

"What's that?" he said.

"It looks like a horse blanket," Max answered, picking the article up from the side of the path they had been following. "Look, it has a name stencilled on it: Fogel Farms. This blanket must belong to that gambler friend of Ferone."

"And that looks like blood!" gulped Marty.

The brothers looked around to make sure their cousin wasn't lying nearby. When they couldn't find him, Marty said, "If he left this blanket behind, he must still be alive, right?"

"I hope so, Marty," said Max. "Let's go back into town and go to the police."

Before they could find the police station, Marty pointed out the window and said, "Whoa! There's a doctor's office. Let's see if he's seen any sign of Barry."

"Good idea," Max said, turning the car into a parking space.

Doc Green had just finished seeing a patient, the last of the day, and his nurse had gone home. When Max and Marty came through the door, he ushered them into his office.

"You fellows look pretty healthy to me," he quipped. "I always look for hockey injuries when I see fellows your age. But you're not limping and you've got all your teeth."

"We're okay," Max said, holding up Barry's photo. "But we're looking for our cousin. We think he's in the area, and we think he's been hurt. He's a husky guy, with blond hair…"

Doc Green leaned forward. He looked at the photo. "I do know a fellow like that. He was beaten up or thrown from a car. I've been treating him for concussion and facial injuries. He's been staying at Ben Fraser's farm, just down the road. If you follow me in your car, I'll take you over to see him. His name is Red Barns."

Max looked at Marty. "Then it's not him," he said, disappointed.

"Let's take a look, anyway," said his brother.

Barry Mitchell's jaw dropped when Doc Green walked into his room at the Fraser farm with Max and Marty at his side.

"How did you two get here?" he asked, his eyes wide.

"We've been looking all over for you, Barry," Max said, obviously concerned. "The whole family is worried about you, especially Bert. Your mom sent us to try and track you down."

"So here we are," Marty piped up. "The great tracers of missing persons!"

"Wait just a minute," said Doc Green, wagging a finger at Barry. "Your name's not Red Barns?"

Barry looked sheepish. "I'm sorry, Doc. I had to give you a fake name. If I hadn't, then the papers might have found out and this room would be full of reporters right now."

"Reporters? Why, what's your real name, young fellow?"

Barry confessed. "I'm Barry Mitchell, the hockey player."

Doc Green leaned over his patient and peered at Barry's face. "Why, so you are," he said. "Those black eyes and that bent nose fooled me. Now you'd better tell me what this is all about."

Barry took a deep breath and told his story. He talked about Nick Ferone and how the man had duped him into thinking he was a good friend. Then he explained how Ferone had him pose for a photo with a notorious gambler and how two thugs had beaten him up and dumped him in the woods wrapped in a horse blanket. Tears flowed from Barry's eyes while he talked.

"I really messed up," he confessed.

"We all mess up when we're young," Doc Green said gently.

"What a horrible friend Nick Ferone turned out

to be," Barry said bitterly. "He turned me against my own brother. And if he gives that photo to the papers, I'll be at the centre of a scandal. My career will be over."

"We'll get that roll of film back," Max said confidently. "Then Ferone and this Fogel guy will have nothing to blackmail you with."

Barry looked dubious. "I don't know how you're going to do that. They're two nasty guys."

CHAPTER 15
A CONFRONTATION IN THE CITY

Barry slept in the back seat of the car almost all the way back to Toronto. When the Mitchell brothers and their cousin reached the city limits, Max stopped the car at a phone booth, nudged Barry awake and asked him for Nick Ferone's telephone number.

Ferone answered on the second ring.

"Mr. Ferone. It's Max Mitchell, remember me?"

"Sure, I remember you."

"I'd like to see you for a minute."

"Not again! I'm pretty busy—I'm going to the track in a few minutes."

"I've got something to show you, Mr. Ferone. It's important. If you don't agree to meet with me, my next call will be to the police. They'll be at your door in 20 minutes. Or they'll pick you up at the racetrack. Wouldn't that be embarrassing, Mr. Ferone?"

Max waited for an answer. Finally it came.

"All right, come around to my house. But be quick about it. And then get out of my life—and stay out this time!"

Minutes later, Max parked by the curb just down the road from Ferone's house. He turned to Barry. "You stay here. We don't want him to see you. Marty and I will handle this."

The boys knocked on Ferone's front door. Max was holding a shopping bag under his arm. Ferone came to the door and grudgingly ushered them in. He was belligerent and intimidating.

"So I'll bet whatever you nosey kids have to show me won't interest me. You're wasting your time."

"Let's go in the kitchen," Max suggested. "The light's probably better in there."

Ferone shrugged, and they moved into the kitchen. A plate sat on the table next to an empty glass. Ferone had been eating a slice of blueberry pie.

"Let's get this over with," Ferone said harshly. "What's up?"

Max pulled the bloodstained blanket from the shopping bag.

"Recognize this, Mr. Ferone?" he asked calmly. "It's the horse blanket you and your men wrapped around Barry Mitchell's body. We found it in the woods near Boonville. It's even got a name stencilled on it—Fogel Farms."

Ferone turned white and was almost speechless. He stared hard at the blanket, and his hands began to shake. *The blanket must have come from Barry Mitchell's dead body,* he thought. *How could these dumb kids possibly have found it?* He tried to compose himself.

"That's got nothing to do with me," he argued. "It means nothing."

"Oh, yes, it does," Max persisted. "This blanket belongs to Fats Fogel, and everyone knows how tight you two are. We figure you ordered your goons to wrap my cousin Barry in this blanket. You told them to dispose of him and to throw his body in the woods outside of Boonville."

Ferone forced himself to laugh. "That's bull!" he said. His eyes narrowed. "Why didn't you go to the cops if that's what you believe? Why come here?"

"We may go to the police," Max told him. "But first we want something from you. We want the roll of film you had the other day—with Barry's photos on it."

"Sorry, I sent it out. It's being processed."

"We don't believe you, Mr. Ferone." Max turned to his brother. "Marty, take a look around."

Marty began moving around the kitchen, looking in various places. When Nick Ferone moved to intercept him, Max stepped in front of him, went chest to chest with the man and stared him in the face. Ferone saw Max's determined look and blinked, then backed down.

"I'll charge you kids with trespassing," he threatened. "And with robbery if you take one thing from this house."

Marty was opening drawers next to the kitchen sink. "Eureka!" he cried, plucking a roll of film from among the knives and forks. "This must be it."

"It's not," shouted Ferone. "It's my... they're my... my wedding photos. Put that film back!"

"Liar!" exclaimed Max. "Barry said you were single."

While Marty held up the film, Max was distracted. Ferone moved fast. He reached into his pocket and pulled out a small revolver.

"Put your hands up!" he shouted, aiming the barrel of the gun directly at Max's head. Slowly, Max and Marty raised their hands.

"Come over here, punk!" Ferone snarled at Marty. "Give me that film!"

Marty handed over the roll. Ferone put it in his pocket. Then, moving quickly again, he grabbed Marty around the neck and pulled him close. He waved the gun at Max.

"You boys are coming with me," he told them. "We'll get in my car and I'll take you for another long ride. So what if you found your stupid cousin's body in the woods. It must still be there, or the news would have been all over the radio and in the papers. Now let's go!"

Ferone snatched up a winter jacket that had been hanging over a chair. He laid it over his arm, hiding the gun. Obediently, Max and Marty preceded him out the front door. He looked both ways before ordering them to move to the front of the garage.

"Open the door," he commanded. Max glanced out toward the curb where the blue Chev was parked. There was no sign of Barry. He was probably asleep in the back seat.

Max hoisted the garage door open and heard it squeal on the runners. "It needs a little grease, Nick," he said.

"Don't get smart with me, kid," Ferone said venomously.

There was a black four-door sedan inside the garage. Ferone pushed the gun into Max's ribs— hard. "You punks get in front." He handed Max the car keys. "You'll drive. I'll sit in back and watch your every move."

"What are you going to do with us?" Marty croaked. He was frightened.

"Well, you punks found out about your cousin's murder. I don't know how you did it, but you should have left well enough alone. It's my lucky day that you didn't go straight to the cops. And it's too late now. I'll tell you this—I'd be stupid to leave any witnesses, wouldn't I? And I'll burn that blanket so there'll be no evidence. Now get in the car."

Max and Marty slid into the front seat. Ferone waited outside, watching them like a hawk.

When they were settled, he opened the door to the back seat and took a step inside. Suddenly, he felt a large hand grip his shoulder. Another hand plunged into his back. He found himself shoved violently face first into the back seat of the sedan. The gun flew from his hand, struck the far door and fell to the floor. He was fumbling for it when his right arm was yanked roughly behind his back. He cried out in pain. He glanced over his shoulder and saw a man with swollen eyes and a taped nose. The man had a murderous look on his face.

"What the..." he stammered. "Let me go! Who are you?"

"Hello, Nick," a smooth voice replied. "Don't you recognize me? It's your old buddy Barry. Now crawl back out of the car and we'll have a friendly chat. Marty will find your gun."

Max sprang from the vehicle. Marty fished in the back seat and came up with the gun.

"I'll get some rope," Max said. "There's some

hanging here in the garage. We'll tie Nick up and bring him in the house, and then we'll call the police. Maybe Nick was right. We probably should have done that in the first place."

"Anyway, we got the film back," Marty said after retrieving it from Nick Ferone's pocket. "What'll I do with it?"

"See if there are any good pictures on it," Max suggested.

Marty took the roll and pulled the end of the film out of the spool until it stopped unrolling. He held it up to the light and squinted. "Nope," he said, grinning. "Not a single photo came out. You're a lousy photographer, Nick."

When the police knocked on Nick Ferone's half-open front door a few minutes later, they heard someone call, "Come in!" They were surprised at the scene they saw in the kitchen. Four men were sitting around the kitchen table. One was bound to a chair with thick rope. The other three were eating—enjoying heaping portions of Mrs. Fitcher's blueberry pie.

CHAPTER 16

BARRY REVEALS ALL

"Well, that wasn't too difficult," Barry Mitchell said as he left the police station with his cousins Max and Marty. "The detective I talked to turned out to be a big hockey fan. He has two kids, and I signed some autographs for them."

"What did he tell you?" Marty asked. Max and Marty had been told to wait outside the room where Barry had been interviewed.

"He told me that charges would be laid against Nick Ferone. Probably attempted murder and kidnapping. The two thugs who took me up to Boonville have already been brought in for questioning. They turned on Nick and blamed him for everything. Of course, they'll be charged as well."

"Will the police go after Fats Fogel?" Max asked.

"They're going to try and charge him with attempting to fix sports events. But he's a slippery guy. If Nick tells them all he knows, they may have a solid case."

"What about you, Barry? Are you in trouble for associating with those two guys, Ferone and Fogel?"

Barry smiled. "The detective thinks I'll be all right. I told him how naive I was—stupid even—to think Ferone was my friend. I was a fool. I admit that. I really messed up. The detective agreed with me, but he didn't think I'd be charged with anything. Still, he warned me to be more careful in the future. He said I should be a good role model for his two kids. He pointed out that associating with gamblers almost cost me my life. I promised him I'd never do such a stupid thing again."

"That's good news," Max said. "I guess we can breathe easier now."

Barry frowned. "Not yet," he said. "Even if the police give me a clean slate, I've still got the NHL to worry about. Mr. Calder, the president, will suspend me in a minute if he finds out I've been associating with gamblers. I'm glad that photo of me with Fats Fogel never got in the papers. I've got you to thank for that."

"Still, Mr. Calder is bound to find out that you made some bad choices," Max said.

Barry grunted. "That's true, now that this has become a police matter. I don't know what to do. I may never play hockey again."

"I know what I'd do if I were you," Max said.

"What?"

"I'd go see Mr. Calder."

Barry decided to follow his cousin's advice. That afternoon, he made an appointment with the league president, stressing the urgency of the situation, and was ushered into his office late in the day. Max and Marty accompanied him. Squint Walker was there too, called in by the president to represent the Leafs.

"Where in the world have you been?" asked Squint once they were settled around a gleaming conference table. "We've been worried sick about you."

"It's a long story," Barry replied. "And now I want to get it off my chest."

Barry spent the next 40 minutes talking about his relationship with Nick Ferone and the circumstances that led to his kidnapping and near murder. He mentioned how ashamed he was when he realized that he'd let so many people down—his brother, his team, his folks, his fans. So ashamed that he didn't want anyone to know his true identity after he was nearly murdered.

Mr. Calder listened intently. Then he came right to the point. "Barry, did you ever, at any time, wager on the outcome of hockey games?" he asked.

"No, sir, I didn't. I would never do that."

"Did you at any time receive a cash payment from a known gambler?"

"No, sir, I didn't."

"Tell me this, young man. I watch a lot of hockey. After a good start this season, I noticed the quality of your performance with the Leafs tailed off. Was that because you were deliberately playing poorly in order for someone else—a gambler perhaps—to profit from your mistakes?"

Barry was shocked. "No, sir," he said emphatically. "I played poorly because I was messing up away from the rink, and I wouldn't listen. I was becoming a celebrity. I was getting a big ego. I enjoyed the attention I was getting from Nick Ferone and his friends. I stayed out late at night, smoking and drinking. I even began arguing with my twin brother—I really regret that. Our teamwork suffered on the ice. My brother and Mr. Walker tried to warn me, but I scoffed at them. I'm really, really sorry I caused so much trouble."

"Do you think you've learned your lesson?" Mr. Calder asked.

"Absolutely!" said Barry.

"Then I've heard enough. I'll render my decision tomorrow."

By the following morning, Barry Mitchell's name was on the front page of all the newspapers.

Attempted Murder of Hockey Star Revealed
Leaf Defenceman Connected
to Gambling Plot

Rookie defenceman Barry Mitchell of the Leafs is fortunate to be alive today. Reported missing several days ago, he turned up yesterday battered and bruised and claiming to be the victim of a botched murder plot. An acquaintance, Nick Ferone, has been arrested by local police and charged with counts of kidnapping and attempted murder. Two other men have also been arrested, and another, Fats Fogel, is under investigation.

Ferone has been interrogated by Toronto police in what may turn out to be a sensational gambling scandal. Ferone stated he "knows nothing" about Mitchell's claim that Ferone took photos of him with Fats Fogel, a well-known gambler. The young hockey star told police that Ferone threatened to send the photos to the newspapers if Mitchell did not co-operate on the ice by playing poorly and thereby affecting the outcome of Leaf hockey games.

Mitchell was found by his teenage cousins Max and Marty Mitchell in Boonville, where he was recuperating in a farmhouse 100 miles north of the city. He had been badly beaten and left in the woods, allegedly by two Ferone accomplices, Joe Phlugg and Nat "Nasty" Newton. Phlugg and Newton have confessed to the crime, but claim that Ferone engineered it.

"My cousin Barry suffered a concussion and maybe some memory loss," said Max Mitchell. "He was well cared for by the Fraser family in Boonville, who took him in. Doc Green of Boonville came to see him every day."

"And he's innocent of any wrongdoing," added Marty Mitchell.

Leaf manager Squint Walker, speaking on behalf of the Leaf organization, stated: "We are relieved and excited that Barry had been found. Those cousins of his did some smart detective work to find him. His safe return means a lot to the Leaf organization. Barry was planning to report to Rochester when the kidnapping took place. We hope he'll resume his career with our minor-league club and be back with the Leafs in the very near future."

When the Leaf executive was reminded that NHL president Calder might suspend his rookie defenceman for associating with high-profile gamblers, Walker admitted, "That's true, he might. I hope he doesn't. We'll just have to wait and see."

Calder's ruling came down later that day. At a press conference, he announced, "I have reached a decision in the case of Leaf player Barry Mitchell. Mitchell asked to meet with me yesterday. During our meeting he was candid and, I believe, sincere and honest. Mitchell admitted to me that he had associated with at least one gambler, namely Nick Ferone. If he associated with other gamblers it was unknowingly. He told me that he knew Mr. Ferone placed wagers at the track and engaged in games of poker, but it wasn't until this week that Mitchell alleges Mr. Ferone tried to persuade him to fix hockey games. And when he refused, Mitchell almost paid for it with his life. As quickly as he was able to, Mitchell reported all of the circumstances to me. I find the player Barry Mitchell to be innocent of any knowing involvement in any attempted fix. He is free to play hockey again in the Leaf organization."

Max and Marty cheered when they heard the news. They were at Union Station, waiting to board the afternoon train to the North Country. Barry had come to see them off and he, of course, was elated. "It's like the weight of the world has been lifted off my shoulders," he stated.

"What now, Barry?" Marty asked.

"Well, I've got my own train to catch in about an hour," he said. "I'm off to Rochester. I'll be working out with my new team tomorrow. And I can't wait to see Bert again."

CHAPTER 17

MEETING A FIGURE SKATER

Bert Mitchell had already played a couple of games with Rochester when his twin brother arrived in town. Bert had been playing well, just a shade off his big-league form. When he heard that Barry was on his way, Bert called the front desk at his hotel. "I'll need a bigger room," he said. "One with two double beds. My brother will be bunking in with me."

"Would you like to book the bigger room for the rest of the season?" the desk clerk asked.

"Heck, no. My brother and I don't expect to be using it for more than a few days."

Then he threw on his jacket and headed for the train station. Perhaps only identical twins can experience the special emotions one feels for the other, feelings that begin before the earliest child-hood memory. Today, Bert felt elated. And he was certain that Barry, en route to Rochester by train, felt exactly the same way.

When Bert met Barry at the train station, they hugged each other as only twins can, as if they'd just won the lottery. Barry was the first to speak, and he began with an apology. But he got no further than, "Brother, I'm sorry..." before Bert interrupted.

"Hush, none of that. I don't need to hear it. Next week, maybe, or after the season. But not now. We've got a game against Cleveland tomorrow. Let's go eat and talk about how we're going to wallop the Barons. Then we can go work out at the arena. You'll need to get your skating legs back."

At the arena after lunch, Bert put Barry through his paces with no heavy equipment and no pucks, just sweatsuits and sticks. For an hour, Barry skated laps, digging in hard for half the length of the ice, then coasting around the net and digging in hard again. He broke into a sweat and was breathing hard before Bert called a halt.

"Let's take a break. We can sit on the players' bench," Bert suggested.

When they skated to the player's bench, part of it was occupied. A young woman in a figure skating outfit was sitting there. She'd been watching them work out. She had dark hair tied in a ponytail, a trim figure and the bluest eyes the twins had ever seen. Bert nodded and murmured hello but Barry moved right in and sat next to her.

He began chatting to her like a used-car salesman.

"Hi there! We didn't see you sitting here. Of course, all the lights aren't on. Are you a figure skater?"

"Yes, I am. I'm on the ice next."

"You are? Gee, I hope we didn't cut it up too much."

The young woman smiled. "I'm sure it's fine. I do most of my routine in the centre ice area."

Barry smiled back. "Do you mind if I watch? I love watching figure skating. There was a girl back home—when I was a kid. She was a figure skater. I had a big crush on her, but I was too shy to tell her. She went away and I never saw her again."

The young woman laughed. "You can watch. It's only fair—I just watched you skating, after all. You're fast."

"Thanks. I'm getting ready to play in the game tomorrow against Cleveland. I've been sent down by the Leafs. Do you want to come to the game? I'm sure my brother can get you a ticket. Can't you, Bert?"

"Sure," said Bert. He nudged Barry with the blade of his stick. "I'm going back. Are you coming?"

"I'll be right there," Barry said. "Wait for me in the coffee shop."

When Barry turned back to the girl, she had a strange look in her eye. "I just figured it out," she said. "You must be Barry Mitchell. I was just reading about you in the local paper. You're one of the Kapuskasing Kids."

Barry threw his arms in the air, as if surrendering. "I am," he admitted. "So you follow hockey?"

"I do. I always have—I'm from the North Country, after all."

"Really? I assumed you lived here in Rochester."

"No, I'm here because this is where the best coach I know lives. I'm staying at her house. I'm entered in the North American championships next week in Michigan."

"Really? What kind of an event is that?" asked Barry.

"It's held every other year for skaters from Canada and the United States. This time it's in the States, so the next one will be in Canada."

"Wait a minute," Barry said, his brows knitted. "You say you're from the North Country? You're not from Kapuskasing by any chance?"

She giggled. "I was. My family moved to Haileybury when I was young."

"You're not... you couldn't be... well, maybe you are... tell me you're not Brenda Fitsell, the girl I had such a crush on when I was 12."

She turned and gave him a dazzling smile. "That's me," she said. "Small world, isn't it?"

Another memory flashed through Barry's mind,

of the Mitchell–McCoy fundraising game in Cobalt.

"We played a game on New Year's Day in Cobalt. The Mitchells against the McCoys. We passed some figure skaters in the corridor, who were waiting to go on the ice. One in particular stood out—she looked familiar. She had a red bow in her hair, and I thought I might meet her after the game. Was that... could that have been...?"

Another wonderful smile. "That was me," Brenda said, leaning back and clapping her hands together. "I remember wearing a red bow that day."

In the coffee shop, Bert finished his coffee and looked at his watch. He tapped his fingers on the table. Then he got up and looked through the glass doors leading into the arena. There on the ice was Barry and the figure skater.

She was holding Barry's hockey stick and he was teaching her how to shoot the puck. When she missed the net after three tries, they began laughing. Then she showed Barry a couple of figure skating moves. She skated backwards, stopped and began to twirl on her skates. She did it effortlessly. Then she stood aside, hands on her hips, and watched while Barry tried. "Piece of cake," Barry said confidently. "Here goes." He skated backwards, stopped, tried to twirl and fell flat on his backside, sliding along the ice until he thumped into the end boards. Laughing, she skated over and helped him to his feet. They began skating arm in arm around the ice.

Bert went back and ordered another coffee.

Moments later, when Barry burst into the coffee shop, Bert thought his twin looked like a cat who'd just stumbled into a roomful of mice.

"Bert! Bert! That girl, the figure skater—that's Brenda Fitsell from back home. Do you remember her? I had such a crush on her. And she's here. Can you believe it?"

Bert blew across the top of his coffee cup. "Sure, I believe it. I remember the crush you had on her, but I didn't remember her name."

"You saw her—she's gorgeous," Barry gushed. "And she wants to come to the game tomorrow. I told her you'd leave a ticket for her at the box office. You will, won't you?"

"I'll do better than that," his brother promised. "I'll leave two tickets."

"Two tickets?"

"Sure. One for her, and the other for her boyfriend."

"Her boyfriend!" Barry's heart fell and his smile faded. He hadn't considered that she might have a boyfriend.

"Yep, her boyfriend," Bert said, his face grim. "I saw her here yesterday with a big hunk of a guy. He looked like a movie star and was built like a wrestler. He gave her a big hug and a kiss."

Barry was stricken. He turned and dashed back into the arena, then came rushing back a minute later. "You liar!" he yelled, punching Bert on the arm, almost spilling his coffee. "Brenda said she wasn't here yesterday. And she swore she doesn't have a boyfriend."

Bert grinned. "Sorry. It must have been somebody else I saw."

Barry Mitchell's three-game stint with the Rochester club in the American League was one of the highlights of the minor-league season. Rochester won three games in a row—twice against league-leading Cleveland, plus a romp over Hershey. With Barry shoring up the defence, playing alongside his brother, Rochester limited their three opponents to a mere two goals. And on offence, Barry was a terror. He made several rink-length dashes that resulted in a goal in each game. And after each goal, he scooped up the puck and presented it to a lovely young woman sitting at rinkside.

A radio announcer high in the booth soon caught on. "Mitchell's giving those pucks to the figure skater Brenda Fitsell," he told his audience. "She's got a chance for a gold medal next week in the championships in Ann Arbor, Michigan."

Barry's black eyes had faded, his nose had almost healed and when he looked in the mirror, he grinned. "Brenda's right," he said out loud. "You are a handsome guy. And you're a very lucky guy."

He and Brenda spent a lot of time together. The crush he'd had on her years earlier was back in full flame. And she, in turn, was charmed by the husky hockey player.

When Rochester manager Bill Claxton reported to Squint Walker on Barry's progress, he was ecstatic. "Leave him with me for the rest of the season, Squint. And his brother, too. They're the best defencemen in the league. We captured a playoff spot last night, mainly because of the Kapuskasing Kids."

"Has Barry been behaving himself—off the ice I mean?"

"Like a choirboy. He's even got himself a girl-friend."

"I wish I could leave them with you, Bill," Squint replied, "but the Leafs need help on the blue line. We've had a couple of injuries. I plan to reunite the Kids with our team—I'm hoping they'll click up here like they did early in the season. If they do, we may be able to take a run at the Stanley Cup."

"So you want me to send them back to Toronto? Just when I was ready to adopt them and write them into my will?"

"Yep, right away."

When Claxton hung up the phone, he sighed. "I'll sure miss those kids. How are we gonna win without them?"

CHAPTER 18

BACK TO THE NHL

The last few games heading into the Stanley Cup playoffs were frantic ones. The Leafs needed a pair of road wins over Montreal and Boston on the final weekend to qualify. They were relying heavily on a pair of rookie defenceman who had been called back from the minors.

Fans and reporters alike expressed surprise at the steady play of the Mitchell brothers in the Saturday night game against the Habs. The twins handed out a number of stiff checks, skillfully cleared the puck out of the zone and covered up nicely for goalie Buddy Broda. Toronto outshot the Habs and won handily 3–1.

It was a much tougher assignment against the Bruins on the following afternoon. Bruins fans were incensed when the Kapuskasing Kids sandwiched Boston ace Eddie Shore early in the game and sent him cartwheeling in the air. A chorus of boos rained down when no penalty was called.

Were the twins intimidated?

"Let's smack him again," Barry said to Bert. "Next chance we get."

"I love to hear these fans howl," was Bert's reply.

They smacked Shore again, and a third time, and the fans went wild. They threw programs and shoe rubbers and other missiles at the Kids. Barry was even hit with a pair of panties and skated cheerfully to the penalty box with the lingerie draped over his head.

While Barry was in the box, Bert blocked a shot on goal, sprang away on a solo dash and scored the only goal of the game. When the game ended, Shore charged across the ice to get at Bert, who failed to see him coming.

But Barry did. He stuck his stick out and tripped the Boston veteran. Shore fell heavily into the boards, staggered to his feet and looked around. He was dazed. Barry helped him to his feet and pumped his hand. "Nice game, Eddie," he said with a smile. "How's the family?"

Shore mumbled, "Pretty good, I guess. Say, which way to our dressing room, anyway?"

The Leafs were in the playoffs!

The momentum from their weekend victories was still with them in the first round of the play-offs. The Leafs polished off the Rangers in four games and waited anxiously for the winner of the Detroit–Chicago series to be decided. The Bentley brothers and Mosienko sparkled for the Hawks, but the Chicago second-stringers faltered and the Red Wings scraped through, four games to three.

The finals would begin on a Thursday night, with the Wings holding home-ice advantage.

The playoff grind is a gruelling business, and when the Leafs boarded the train for the Motor City most of the players sported various cuts and bruises. Their only consolation was that the Red Wings had similar problems to contend with.

"Both teams feel confident of victory," veteran broadcaster Foster Hewitt told a nationwide radio audience. "Squint Walker's crew is looking stronger now that the Kapuskasing Kids are back from the boondocks and playing well, but the Leafs had some problems late in the season and are considered the underdogs. But Squint says, 'Don't worry about that. We'll take those Wings.'"

Red Wing manager Harry Conklin scoffed at Walker's prediction. "He should leave predictions to the gypsies and the fortune tellers," Conklin snorted. "This has been the Red Wings' greatest season. We'll be guzzling champagne from the Cup in a matter of days."

Conklin appeared to be the better judge of play-off hockey when his Red Wings captured the first two games of the final series in the Detroit Olympia. In the second period of the opener, Barry Mitchell stopped a Slick McCoy slapshot with his ankle and had to leave the game. When Bert and a teammate assisted Barry off the ice, Slick skated by and smirked. "I hope it's broken," he said cruelly. "It's right where I was aiming."

Barry shed tears of frustration while the trainer taped an ice pack to his bruised ankle. "I've got to get back," he told Bert. "I told Brenda I'd score a big goal for her in the finals."

"You can't score if you can't skate," Bert pointed out.

In game two, it was Broda who went down. After two periods of scoreless hockey, a rising shot caught the goalie in the throat. He fell, gagging and choking, pawing the ice like a boxer after taking a kayo punch.

Broda insisted on staying in the game, but it was a foolish decision. His eyes watered, he could hardly breathe and he let in three quick goals.

After the game, the Leafs boarded their train for home, trailing in the series two games to none. There was no horseplay and minimal chatter. The Leafs knew they'd have to win game three on home ice—or else.

And they did! Barry suited up for the game wearing a sponge pad in his skate, protecting his bruised ankle. The team doctor had recommended that Barry have x-rays taken, but he had refused. The ankle pained him, but he managed to play a steady defensive game. He also ignored the taunts of Slick McCoy, who skated past him saying things like, "Hey, Mitchell, do you want me to get you a cane? How about some crutches?"

Late in the game, with the Red Wings leading 3–2, centre Terry Noble silenced Slick and the Red Wings. He took a pass from Barry and went deep in the zone, then sifted out of the corner with time running out to score the tying goal with a wrap-around.

In the first overtime period, Barry Mitchell put his full weight behind a shot from the point. It was a blazing shot that somehow got through a battling mob of players in front of goalie Mower's crease. Mowers stabbed at the puck with his glove and missed. The red light flashed! The Leafs managed their first victory of the finals by a 4–3 score.

Barry was skating with his old-time speed in game four. The bruised ankle still bothered him, but he refused to let it hold him back. He teamed up with Bert to stymie the Red Wings at every turn. And while he did score a goal, it wasn't the big one he'd promised Brenda.

Barry opened the scoring with a rush into the Detroit zone. He drilled a shot at Mowers, who caught it high on his chest, then dropped the rebound in front. Barry raced in and popped the puck into the corner of the net.

But it was Terry Noble who caught the crowd's fancy. He rifled home the second goal, with a spin-around shot that deflected in off the crossbar. Mowers never saw the puck coming. Noble followed up late in the game with a second goal, and later on when the Wings pulled their goalie, he skimmed the puck the length of the ice for an empty-netter. Bert and Barry drew assists on all three of his goals, and the Leafs won 4–1 behind Noble's hat trick.

Series tied 2–2.

Game five would long be remembered for the tenacious checking of both clubs and the out-standing defensive play of both teams. The forwards, leg weary at the end of a long season, failed to muscle through and get their shots away. Playing on home ice, the Red Wings managed one goal to scrape through by a score of 1–0. Broda was quick to praise the Kids after the game.

"They've been rock-solid since they came up from Rochester," he told the *Toronto Star*. "Remember, they're just kids. And they've battled through a whole lot of adversity this season."

Game six! Maple Leaf Gardens was jammed to capacity, with thousands and thousands of excited faces rising in tiers from the rail seats to the peanut gallery. The sheet of ice lay dead white under the gleaming rows of lights. It was an atmosphere of pent-up excitement, with the anticipation of great deeds to be performed. Outside the building, scalpers hawked tickets. "A pair of reds! Get 'em now! Only 100 bucks."

It was crisis time for the visiting Red Wings. Harry Conklin was in a sour mood. He had expected to wrap up the series in four games and be lugging the Stanley Cup around Detroit by now. If his team stumbled tonight, they would have to go to a game seven, and he knew his players were tired. And if they ended up losing the series in a final game on home ice, they would spend the off-season thinking of themselves as second-raters, also-rans, wondering how they'd lost to the hated Leafs.

The players came out now, bright-sweatered figures, looping and darting, looking courageous and confident. A great cheer erupted, then died away, followed by a loud buzz of oohs and aahs and predictions of what might happen.

The teams lined up. The crowd rose as the strains of the national anthem broke the sudden hush. Another wave of noise erupted as the anthem died away. The players slapped each goalie's pads with their sticks and went to their benches. The netminders moved back and forth, roughing up the ice in their creases, then crouched, watching and waiting for the puck to drop.

The referee threw the puck down and the centres clashed their sticks over it, Terry Noble versus Slick McCoy. The disc squirted loose, back to the Detroit defence. The game was underway.

Bert and Barry Mitchell skated gracefully back to their blue line, anticipating a fast opening period full of brilliant attacks, solid defensive play and stellar goaltending. And that's exactly what they got.

The Red Wings' offence was carried by Slick McCoy, who came up with a dozen clever plays and some expert passing. But the Leaf defence thwarted him when he came in close. Bert knocked the puck off his stick on one foray, and Barry nailed him with a hip check on another, sending him sliding into the end boards. The ovation Barry got was deafening. Slick was irate and screamed for a penalty. When the referee shook his head, Slick called him a dirty so-and-so.

"What did you say?" the referee asked.

"Nothing," Slick mumbled, avoiding a trip to the box.

The Kids thoroughly tied up McCoy in the opening period, disrupting the effectiveness of the Red Wings' number one line. But if there was an edge in play, it belonged to the Wings.

It was more of the same in the second period. Neither team could score, but there were plenty of close calls and both goaltenders were heroic.

In the second intermission, Coach Irvin gave a pep talk that ended with, "You can do it, boys! You can do it! I know you can, and you know you can."

He turned to the Kids as the players filed out. "Wear Slick McCoy down if you can. Stay with him. Run him ragged. If you see a scoring chance, grab it, but don't take foolish chances."

Midway through the third period, the Kids could see they were getting to McCoy, getting his goat. He had tried every trick he knew to get around them, to find room to send crisp passes to his teammates or to score himself, unleashing his big shot. But there was no room. There were no big shots. He was bumped and jostled and sent spinning. When Barry rode him hard into the boards, he exploded. "You busher!" he howled. "I'll teach you!" He lashed out with his stick and smashed Barry viciously across his shin pads, knocking his feet out from under him.

The whistle blew. "Two minutes for slashing!" barked the referee. McCoy slowly made his way to the box, head down, knowing his loss of self-control could cost his team the game.

With the man advantage, the Leafs sprang to the attack. Bert and Barry stayed out on the ice, taking a long shift, making swift passes to hard-charging teammates.

Inside the Red Wing zone, the best passers and shooters moved the puck around smoothly. It moved from man to man, and finally it came to Bert. In five seconds, McCoy would be charging out of the box. Bert faked a shot, then slid the puck smoothly across the ice to Barry. Barry one-timed the puck high and hard toward the net. It soared, brushed a Red Wing jersey in flight, zipped by the thrust of a defenceman's stick and slammed into the net.

When the red light flashed, an incredible din filled the building. It was so loud that no one heard the snap of Slick McCoy's stick breaking when he smashed it in rage against the door of the penalty box.

A minute later, the game ended. The Leafs had forced a seventh game. It would be played two nights later, back in Detroit.

Barry made a beeline for Mowers' net. Mowers had left the cage and collared the puck. He held it in his big glove and tried to brush past Barry.

"I want that puck!" Barry called out, blocking Mower's path. "It's the one I scored with."

"I want it too," Mowers said. "I'm retiring after the final game, so this may be the last goal ever scored against me."

"But it's more important to me, Johnny," Barry pleaded. "And I'll score another against you back in Detroit, I promise. Then that one can be your last."

Mowers saw the absurdity of Barry's offer. "I'd rather you not score on me in Detroit," he muttered. He opened his glove and turned over the puck.

CHAPTER 19
THE FINAL BATTLE FOR THE CUP

In game seven, the roar of the crowd, the red and white banners and the stamping of several thousand feet signalled full support for the home team. Manager Harry Conklin looked up at the throng and said, "We'll bring you the Stanley Cup tonight." Conklin figured a roaring crowd would mean at least one goal for his team. The fans expected an epic clash, one of those spectacular games that go down in hockey history. Some came armed with eggs and rotten fruit that they would throw on the ice if the visitors took a lead, or to celebrate a goal, or whenever else they felt like causing trouble. One had even brought a slimy octopus. Anything to disrupt the hated Leafs.

The puck was dropped and the final game of the season got underway. The opening period alone was worth the price of admission. Both teams attacked furiously, striving for the all-important first goal. Both goaltenders were peppered with shots and both were called upon to stop a pair of breakaways. Slick McCoy came close to scoring in the final minute of the period when he rang a shot off the goal post.

The second period was equally spectacular, with a dozen close calls at each goalmouth. Enough bodies were slapped down by thumping bodychecks to satisfy a wrestling crowd. Both teams' forwards checked back fiercely, while their defencemen rode opponents into the boards with tooth-rattling checks. Fans sitting ten rows back could hear the grunts and groans when players collided, when scoring chances were missed.

Bert and Barry were in the thick of it, breaking up plays and sending well-timed passes to forwards in full flight. Slick McCoy barrelled into Bert and knocked him to the ice. And when the referee turned his back, McCoy elbowed Bert in the face, bloodying his nose and sending him reeling. McCoy laughed and scurried away when Barry came charging over.

Bert had to leave the ice, as blood splattered over his jersey. While he was off, McCoy slipped through and blasted a shot past Broda. The Red Wings had the first goal. Programs, peanuts, hot dogs and half a dozen eggs flew from the stands and hit the ice. One egg soiled the jersey on Broda's broad back. The Leaf goalie glared up at the crowd. It was bad enough to give up a goal. He didn't need to be used as a target for imbecilic egg-tossers.

"How do you like that?" McCoy taunted Barry as the Red Wing glided back to centre ice. "Pretty, huh?"

"You're pretty, McCoy," Barry fired back. "Pretty pathetic."

Before the period ended, McCoy swept in again, this time when the twins were on the bench. He stormed right in on Broda and slammed him backwards into the net. McCoy's linemate shovelled the puck over the goal line when Broda stumbled and fell. The light flashed and the referee—a Detroiter—nodded. "Good goal," he ruled, while the Leafs screamed for an interference call.

The visitors trailed by two at the end of 40 minutes.

Broda complained of a sore back during the intermission, and Bert's nose was badly swollen.

"That McCoy!" railed the coach. "He's as mean and nasty as any player I've ever seen. But we've got one more period, boys. Twenty minutes to get back in this game."

There wasn't much more chatter. The Leafs had failed to get the puck past Mowers, and their Stanley Cup hopes were slipping away. And they'd have to rely on a goalie with a wonky back when they skated back out for the final time.

In the third period, Broda was once again showered with debris. Then he was forced to leap aside as a slimy octopus landed on top of his net, bounced off and lay limp on his doorstep.

"Yikes!" he yelled. "Get this thing away from me."

Barry took Bert aside. "If we can stop McCoy, we can still beat these guys," he said. "He's so arrogant. He thinks this game is all wrapped up like a Christmas present."

"I'll send him a present," Bert growled. "I owe him one for this." He pointed to his nose.

Five minutes into the third period, there was a fight. Terry Noble was fouled from behind—a slash across the knees. When no penalty was called, he retaliated. He dropped his gloves and belted Hagman, a huge Red Wing defenceman, in the chops. Hagman punched back, and both players were handed five-minute penalties. With each club playing shorthanded, the game opened up. The speedsters had room to move. And one of them was Barry Mitchell.

We've got to start taking chances, Barry told himself, *or this game will be over and we'll be thinking of what might have been.*

He took a cross-ice pass from Bert, avoided an

incoming checker and darted straight up centre. Another Red Wing forward shifted over and tried to knock Barry off stride. The Leaf rookie held the man off, scooted over the blue line and shot the puck all in one motion.

Surprised by the quickness of the blast, Mowers leaped in front of the puck and threw his glove at the flying rubber. But it was too late—the puck was already in the net. The Leafs were finally on the board.

Broda slapped his big goal stick on the ice. "One more, kid, one more!" he shouted.

Slick McCoy came out for the faceoff at centre. He gave Barry a mock salute with his glove. "You lucky stiff! Watch me get that one back."

McCoy won the draw and barrelled in. He'd show the Kids a move or two that would make them burn with embarrassment.

He shifted at the blue line, slowed and then turned into the inviting gap between Bert and Barry. If he was quick about it, there was just enough room to slip through. McCoy put on a burst and leaped into the hole when...

Whap!

His whole world came crashing down. Bert and Barry moved effortlessly together and closed the gap. Their timing was perfect. Bert slammed into Slick with a shoulder while Barry upended him with a solid hip check. Slick's stick went flying and his gloves came off. He hit the ice with a thud that could be heard as far away as Kalamazoo. And while he lay gasping, sprawled on the ice, Bert calmly picked up the puck and started away with it.

He drilled a pass up to Blair, who skimmed the puck right back to him. Bert was in full flight when he crossed the Detroit blue line. He faked a pass back to Blair, who went wide, then cut in smoothly behind the defenceman. Bert waited for Blair to get clear, and when he did, he lobbed a pass through the defence. The puck landed squarely on the blade of Blair's stick and he slammed it past Mowers before the goalie could blink.

Tie game!

The twins looked up at the big clock over centre ice. Forty seconds to play.

"We'll get them in overtime," Bert shouted at Barry. "Don't let them get another shot."

"There isn't going to be an overtime! Get me the puck and I'll end it," his brother shouted back.

Twenty seconds later, Broda trapped a loose puck in behind his net. He shovelled it into the corner to Bert, who wheeled and was about to hoist it high into the centre ice zone, killing time, when he saw Barry breaking fast, uncovered, shouting, "Here, Bert, here!"

Bert skimmed a pass up the ice to Barry, who cradled it, then took off like a stallion.

One Red Wing forward clawed at his jersey, then stumbled and fell. Another leaped in front of Barry, but the rookie slipped the puck through his legs, left him spinning and picked the puck up again.

The Red Wing defencemen backed in over their blue line. Ten seconds to play. Barry pulled the puck back, lining up his shot. A defender went down to block, protecting his face with his glove.

Seven seconds to play.

Barry took a quick glance behind him. His teammates were scrambling to catch up, but they would be too late. He would have to make a last-gasp effort on his own.

Five seconds.

He leaped over the fallen Red Wing, somehow pulling the puck through with him. The other defenceman lunged at him, missed and fell, clutched at his leg. Barry sensed that time was running out. He would have to shoot—now!

Two seconds.

His strong wrists propelled the puck at Mowers, who was moving out, desperate to cut down the angle to his net. Barry groaned, figuring he had aimed too wide. But the puck struck the knob of

Mower's goal stick, changed direction slightly and flew into the net behind him.

A lucky goal, but the winning goal!

Barry threw his arms high in the air, shouted "Yoweee!" at the top of his lungs and did a little step dance. He had scored in the final second of play.

His teammates pounced on him, those on the ice and others who leaped off the bench. They laughed and shouted, pounded his back, knocked him down and yanked him back to his feet again. They pulled off his gloves to shake his hand. Blair gave him a kiss on the cheek. Bert embraced him and shouted in his ear, "What a comeback, brother! You're a hero! A Stanley Cup hero!"

The Detroit fans swallowed their disappointment and raised their voices in a cheer for their beloved Red Wings. They cheered again for the new champions, then stood and applauded when president Calder called the Leafs to centre ice for the Cup presentation. A red carpet was rolled out and suddenly, there it was—the Stanley Cup, the symbol of hockey supremacy since 1894.

After Calder's traditional congratulatory speech, the Cup was hoisted in the air, first by Blair, then by Broda and then by each of the rest of the victorious team. When it was their turn to embrace the gleaming trophy, Bert and Barry held

it high together. They wanted to celebrate this moment as a pair.

Flashbulbs popped as photographers slipped and slid around the ice, recording the moment for posterity.

And then, out of the corner of his eye, Barry saw someone he never expected to see. He was so surprised that his knees wobbled. There in the gate, waving her arms, was Brenda Fitsell.

Barry skated over and embraced her, kissed her on both cheeks. "What are you doing here?" he gasped. "I thought you were in Ann Arbor?"

"I was. The finals were held this afternoon. Then I rushed over here—Ann Arbor's only a few miles away."

"I'll bet you won the gold," said Barry.

"I did, I did!" said Brenda excitedly.

"That's wonderful news, Brenda. I'm so proud of you! Have you got your medal?"

She pulled open her coat. The gold medal hung from her neck.

"Come on," urged Barry. "Come out on the ice with me. We'll get our photos taken—you with your medal and me with the Cup."

"I can't," she protested. "This is your moment, not mine."

"Of course you can," he argued, and pulled her by the arm, helping her across the ice to where

Bert was holding the Cup. The announcer recognized her and gave Brenda a grand introduction. The fans bellowed their approval as the flashbulbs caught the moment. Barry embraced the Cup with one arm and Brenda with the other, her gold medal gleaming in her hand.

"Don't they look cute?" one photographer said to another.

"Cute? They're more than cute. Why, they look like a couple of kids who are just about to fall in love."

THE REST OF THE STORY

Bert and Barry Mitchell returned to Kapuskasing a month later with the Stanley Cup resting on the back seat of Bert's blue Chev. President Calder had allowed the trophy to accompany the twins. He'd offered the Calder Trophy as well, which he'd awarded to Bert Mitchell as rookie of the year in a post-season ceremony.

"No, I'll leave that one in Toronto," Bert had said. "It doesn't mean as much if Barry can't share it with me."

"But there can only be one winner," Calder had told him. "And your brother did have a troubled season. He was a close second."

"Bring it," Barry had told him. "You deserve it, not me."

"No," Bert had insisted. "It's enough that we have the Stanley Cup."

A mile-long parade was arranged for the Kapuskasing kids, and on a sunny Saturday morning they found themselves driving through town in the back of a convertible while crowds cheered and waved Maple Leaf banners. Small children ran alongside their car.

In a second convertible, Brenda Fitsell threw kisses to the crowd. Her friends in Kapuskasing

wanted to honour the former resident for her gold-medal performance in figure skating.

Among the spectators were Max and Marty Mitchell, who had driven up from Indian River to visit their NHL cousins. Marty had his camera and took dozens of photos, while Max took notes for a story he was writing about Barry and Bert. It would be published simultaneously in the *Indian River Review* and the *Kapuskasing Mirror*.

The story was picked up by the *Toronto Star*, and two days later Nick Ferone read about the parade in his prison cell. He and his accomplices, Joe Pflugg and Nat Newton, had been convicted of kidnapping and attempted murder and were serving long terms in the penitentiary. When Ferone showed the newspaper to Pflugg and Newton, they merely shrugged. Neither one could read.

Fats Fogel read about the parade while sitting at his kitchen table eating a gourmet meal. The case against him had been dropped for lack of evidence.

After the Stanley Cup celebrations were over, Bert and Barry returned to the city to begin their studies at the University of Toronto. In the university archives one day, Bert looked up a history of the Chicago Black Hawks and discovered that the stories Coach Irvin had told him about Coach

Matheson and goalie Charlie Gardiner were true. Most of the other hockey stories—the building of Maple Leaf Gardens, the first game in Montreal, the flu epidemic and Lester Patrick's stories—were also true.

In August, Barry Mitchell announced his engagement to Brenda Fitsell. He bought her a diamond ring with his playoff bonus.

Slick McCoy played part of another season with Detroit, but when he was passed over for the team captaincy, he complained bitterly that he deserved the honour and demanded a trade. Harry Conklin obliged by trading him to the New York Rangers. In New York, he began associating with men involved in criminal activity, some of them professional gamblers. When Slick reneged on a bet, one of the mobsters told a sportswriter that Slick had wagered on hockey games, some of them involving his own team. Following an investigation, President Calder banned him from hockey for life.

And for the tenth consecutive year, Mrs. Fitcher won first prize in the pie-baking contest at the Boonville fall fair.